A DOG'S LIFE

Recent Titles by Gerald Hammond from Severn House

COLD IN THE HEADS
CRASH
DOWN THE GARDEN PATH
THE DIRTY DOLLAR
A DOG'S LIFE
FINE TUNE
THE FINGERS OF ONE FOOT
FLAMESCAPE
GRAIL FOR SALE
HIT AND RUN
THE HITCH
INTO THE BLUE
KEEPER TURNED POACHER
LOVING MEMORY
ON THE WARPATH
THE OUTPOST
A RUNNING JUMP
SILENT INTRUDER
THE SNATCH
WAKING PARTNERS
WELL AND GOOD

A DOG'S LIFE

Gerald Hammond

This first world edition published 2010
in Great Britain and in 2011 in the USA by
SEVERN HOUSE PUBLISHERS LTD of
9–15 High Street, Sutton, Surrey, England, SM1 1DF.
Trade paperback edition first published
in Great Britain and the USA 2011 by
SEVERN HOUSE PUBLISHERS LTD.

British Library Cataloguing in Publication Data

Hammond, Gerald, 1926-
  A dog's life.
  1. Homeless women–Fiction. 2. Novelists–Crimes
Against–Fiction. 3. Murder–Investigation–Fiction.
  4. Detective and mystery stories.
  I. Title
  823.9'14-dc22

ISBN-13: 978-0-7278-6962-3   (cased)
ISBN-13: 978-1-84751-288-8   (trade paper)

All Severn House titles are printed on acid-free paper.

Severn House Publishers support The Forest Stewardship Council [FSC],
the leading international forest certification organisation. All our titles that
are printed on Greenpeace-approved FSC-certified paper carry the FSC logo.

Mixed Sources
Product group from well-managed
forests and other controlled sources
www.fsc.org Cert no. SA-COC-1565
© 1996 Forest Stewardship Council

Typeset by Palimpsest Book Production Ltd.,
Falkirk, Stirlingshire, Scotland.
Printed and bound in Great Britain by
MPG Books Ltd., Bodmin, Cornwall.

ONE

Tim Russell, the novelist, still lives in a pleasant old house (converted from a farmer's feed store), now in the very edge of a village which is on the point of being swallowed by a small town within commuting distance of a city on the east coast of Scotland.

Visitors and even locals are sometimes surprised to see the attachment between Tim and his three-legged chocolate Labrador bitch Umber. They and Mrs Russell form almost a *ménage a trois*. Where the Russells go, the dog goes too. Tim, in particular, hardly ever takes out his gun, but they enjoy picking up on the local shoots where the dog, despite lacking one hind leg, performs very creditably, frequently 'wiping the eye' of gamekeepers' four-limbed animals. Only the occasional wire fence, if it is more that waist high to her master, defeats Umber, forcing her to detour to the nearest gateway. Often Tim will hurry and struggle to lift her over. She is no light weight but he knows that, left to her own devices, she may make a valiant attempt at a fence that requires the use of both hind legs and, failing, rip herself on the top strand of barbed wire. The couple and the dog have reached that level of understanding that it takes no more than the movement of a finger to convey an order; or a pause and an enquiring glance to signify a bird for collection.

The reason for this close attachment deserves to be more widely known. To let the reader understand the background to the story we may go back a very few years.

'Don't go thinking of this as being your fault,' Cecily said. She blew a smoke ring at the ceiling. She had done that a lot over the past two years. There was a sooty circle developing on the ceiling above her head. 'If it's anybody's fault it's mine. These have been a good couple of years. You've made me comfortable, given me time to think, and the sex has been out of this world. But that isn't enough. A woman with an active mind needs something more demanding. I'm not qualified for a profession, I'm not going to start studying now and I'm damned if I'll settle for a job as a shorthand typist.

'If we'd had babies, now, that might have been different. I can imagine myself devoting my life to raising ungrateful and even resentful children, picking up after them just as I do for you, wiping their noses and never a word of thanks until I'm too old to give a damn.' She wriggled herself into an even more comfortable position on the settee. 'That could have been a fulfilling life. But it seems that we can't make babies together. I didn't understand everything that specialist told us, but it boiled down to the fact that your sperm doesn't like my eggs. I'm glad now that we never married.

'I can't see myself settling down to a lifetime of the sort of existence that most well-heeled, childless wives settle for, cooking and cleaning, going to the health club and for beauty treatments, giving little dinner parties, shopping and starting all over again. I've watched them. It leaves them with too much spare mental capacity and damn-all to fill it with. Except for next week's shopping list – and the Internet's made that too damn easy, I just put in the same old list with one or two minor changes and tell it to "send". Next day, a van rolls up.

'I want challenges. I need them. I want what most women dread – squalling babies, sickly toddlers, tearful children, demanding pupils, rebellious teenagers and in the end doctors and lawyers who owe it all to Mum whether they know it or not. Do you see what I mean? Do you?'

She went on without awaiting a reply. She was a fine-looking woman, just beyond the first bounce of girlhood, dark-haired and flashing eyes after the manner of a South American film star.

'And I'll tell you something else. I don't mind a good long hike in the country. I will say that you get along well for a man who lost a foot and part of a leg in a motorbike smash. But my great pleasure was in tennis and I was good at it, but it's beyond you. I can't blame you for that. The judge decided that the lorry was at fault and you got your compensation, but that only means that you don't have to work if you don't want to. You do want to, but your work is writing which means that I have you under my feet for most of the day without having your company. All right, so you're a mid-list novelist and you tell me often enough that the money pays for the cruises. Well, cruises are boring too. The people are boring, the places are boring and the days at sea are the most boring of all. You're company of a sort, or you would be if you ever said anything.

'I have to tell you that the time has come for major changes. I met up with some of our friends yesterday evening while you were at the gym. Your friends as much as mine, believe it or not. And after the wine had flowed a little, one of those conversations began that only happen once in a blue moon. A moment of revelation in which people say what they really think without reservations, frankly and openly and cheerfully instead of between the sheets and in whispers. After a few minutes I could hardly believe what I was hearing and yet I had known all along at a certain level that it was true. It began when Fred and Judy told us that they were separating, staying very good friends all the same. But Fred has always fancied Hannah and they're going to live together and eventually marry. And that's when Hugo, rather shyly, admitted that he'd always lusted after me. I won't repeat the whole conversation to you because some of it was confidential and you probably wouldn't believe the rest of it anyway, but he was very frank and almost lyrical and the upshot of it is that I'm going off with Hugo. We both have marriage in mind. It will be very suitable. We like the same things and he's already proved that he can father a baby or two.

'In fact this seemed to set off several other changes of partners, so you'll see a bit of a general post happening over the next few weeks. And of course nothing is ever absolutely tidy. There were bound to be one or two left out at the ends of the chain. And the two wallflowers were you and Fat Alice. I don't suppose you'd fancy her –' Cecily smiled at a remembered pleasure – 'indeed I seem to remember you being rather outspoken on the subject, but I've no doubt that you'll manage all right without me, in fact you'll hardly notice that I've gone, will you? Will you?'

From long habit, Tim had been listening only with that part of his mind that was always alert for dialect, cadence and turns of phrase. He knew that his subliminal reflexes would alert him if her tone changed to suggest that an answer or comment was expected. At other moments he tended to limit his remarks to the essential, for fear of provoking a deluge of barely relevant reply. But the lingering echo of her last few words gave him no clue as to whether the positive or negative was required. There was only one sure and proven avenue of escape. 'What do you think?' he said.

'I doubt it.'

'So do I.'

That, he was soon made to realize, was the wrong answer.

He went for a walk with India, his old black Labrador. Usually they would have turned onto the farmland that neighboured the small, private development, but this time he went the other way, into the village that was becoming a suburb of the neighbouring town. Just round the first bend there was a pub, the Mackillop Arms, and he turned in at the door. India took up her usual place before the dartboard. Tim saw Kenneth Salter, a neighbour and one of the usual group of cronies, standing alone at the bar. Tim was essentially a very shy man, although he had learned to hide the fact behind a veil of courtesy and humour, but Ken came close to being his friend. Ken had indeed been a witness to the discussion that Cecily had described and Tim was soon in possession of the facts with embellishments.

Ken's manner was apologetic, as though he felt that he should perhaps have done something to avert the disruption to Tim's settled existence, but he was assured that the split had been inevitable although a long time coming. They exchanged pints. Tim saw no reason to hurry home but at least it came as no shock to him when he did return much later to the converted building and found that Cecily had been busy. A van must have been called, because not only had all her clothes and other possessions vanished but so also had some expensive kitchen equipment and more than half of his extensive book collection.

He could live without most of the books – they were old friends but they were also a reminder of the myriads of dead and forgotten authors whose numbers he was determined never to join. On the other hand there was also a note to explain that his dinner, now frizzled, was in the oven.

Tim and India did indeed 'manage'. A new routine developed. Tim had become unaccustomed to returning home to a cold and empty house, but what he lost in having to cater for them both he made up in not having to listen, or pretend to listen, to a thousand words from the often garrulous Cecily when ten would have conveyed the message more adequately and been more easily absorbed. For a few months Tim and India were as contented a couple as could be found. Even the celibate existence Tim found acceptable. Sex would only have reminded him of the endless chatter.

Those few months fled by. Then India developed a lump and all too soon the vet was suggesting that the kindest course would be the privilege reserved for animals but forbidden to humans, the sleep of euthanasia. Tim shed a tear, which was more than he had done for the departed Cecily.

The house was now colder and emptier. For the first time in years, Tim began to feel the bite of loneliness. He finished writing his current novel and did not feel settled enough to begin another. Proof-reading the previous one filled a few days. Some female companionship would not have come amiss but his friends all seemed to be neatly paired off and he was too listless and too shy to go on the prowl. Girls seemed to be in short supply. He even went on a cruise, one known as 'The Widow's Cruise', but those widows looking for a second (or fourth or fifth) husband could have been his mother with time to spare.

He returned home convinced that another dog would provide the company he craved and that India would not have grudged him a successor. This conviction was reinforced when he found that his house had been entered in his absence.

His losses were not great. In the knowledge that there had been a spate of burglaries in the district, he never left money in the house. Cecily had removed most of his more extravagant purchases; he had left his shotgun with a friendly gunsmith and taken his laptop computer with him. Any papers that might have been of use to an identity thief had been burned. With the aid of the insurance settlement and a little help from his savings, what was missing could be replaced and even improved. All the same a dog, while being the best of company, makes an excellent burglar alarm.

One may well wonder, looking around, what guides many people to their choice of a dog. Sometimes, of course, the owner's occupation makes the choice of a working breed almost inevitable, but in others the choice seems surely to have been random, arbitrary or even perverse, perhaps as a tribute to some happy childhood memory. The chosen tyke may be smelly, savage, impossible to train, totally unsuited to the owner's residence or lifestyle or even grossly unsightly to the eye of anyone but a devoted master.

Tim had always had a fancy for a chocolate Labrador – despite or perhaps because of the perceived difficulties. Chocolate Labs have a reputation for being difficult to train, so that breeders are reluctant to specialize in them. When a black and a yellow are mated the resultant mixed litter will sometimes include one or two chocolate pups, but Tim, extrapolating from an inadequate sample, had the impression that these, in obedience to some Mendelian law, are usually male. He had always preferred bitches. It happened, however, that a lady of his acquaintance had, due to the carelessness of a visiting teenager in leaving unlatched a kennel door, been presented with a mixed litter containing a chocolate bitch. The lady had tried to jack the price up on grounds of rarity, but Tim pointed out firmly that the Kennel Club would not allow any of the litter to be registered because of the accidental nature of the mating and the uncertainty as to which of the neighbourhood's black Labs was the guilty father, thus preventing them or their descendants from ever being competed or shown. She had countered, with a threatening movement of her imposing bosom, by pointing out that the Kennel Club need not know. Tim had hinted, very delicately, that they damn soon would know unless . . .

He secured the pup for a nominal sum and named her Umber. Then there began the usual halcyon period. Tim reassured, protected and comforted the pup, fed her the best and played with her on the grass. The puppy adjusted to the loss of her immediate family, learned quickly and fell in love with her new master. The safest place in the universe was on or behind or beneath his knees. When the time came for her to be spayed, she even accepted being left at the surgery – she knew that he would come back for her and whatever he wished must be right. He was the infinite provider. He was God.

TWO

By the autumn of the following year, Umber had progressed through the stage of puppyhood and from elementary fetching of tennis balls to carrying or fetching a dummy thrown by hand or fired from a launcher. She had responded, with only occasional hiccups, to commands given by hand signal, whistle or voice. She soon learned that outdoors is the place for defecation and that none of Tim's possessions was for chewing. This last applied particularly to electric wires.

Umber showed some signs of being difficult to train. She was impetuous, but only in her anxiety to do whatever her master wished whether the command had been given yet or not. Tim soon found that what she did learn she never forgot. This led him to be careful that no bad habits were learned from other dogs. He knew from past experience that you can teach a Labrador anything but that to unteach one of them anything once taught verges on the impossible. There were many dogs in the neighbourhood habituated to jumping up, barking without good reason or rolling in or eating the unspeakable. Tim hoped to use her in the shooting field where absolute steadiness is an essential. (A dog that 'runs in' may well be shot. It will certainly disturb the game in areas still to be visited.) But most dogs are sociable and Umber would have been easily tempted to break away from heel. Tim spent several months restricting their walks to the farmland bordering the houses. Even when he was sure that the lesson had been learned, he preferred to start and finish his walks in early morning and late evening when other dog-walkers were in front of the box or safely abed. It was his long-standing habit to go to bed early, sleep like the dead and to rise as soon as he awoke, so early rising was no hardship to him.

Tim's house, which had been built by some early Victorian farmer as a feed store to replace a smaller store nearby, was built of stone and pitch-pine and slates, robust enough to withstand the climate of northern Scotland. Both had been converted into private dwellings just before the Second World War. In the post-war housing boom they had become among the outermost houses of an exclusive housing development. The village was becoming a protruding suburb of what was, after all, not a very large town. Tim's front windows looked along a tree-lined street of well built and individual if sometimes unimaginative houses with proudly tended gardens that exploded into flower in season. His rear windows looked over his own modest garden to a swathe of farmland broken by strips of woodland wherever the ground was unsuitable for the plough. His garden was enclosed by an old stone wall. Making a gate in the wall would have entailed both expense and the bother of obtaining consents from the farmer, the feudal superior, the planning authority and probably God, so Tim had never bothered. His house had become the central one of three fronting on to the hammerhead that terminated the approach road, and there was a path to the farmland accessible between a neighbour's house and one of the houses on the approach road.

On a cool September morning he was heading in that direction accompanied by Umber, with dawn showing as little more than a lessening of the darkness, when he saw a figure approaching. Their paths would converge at the mouth of the path to the farmland so he checked his stride; then, in the growing light, he saw that the other had no dog with him and therefore presented no threat to training. He moved on and as the distance lessened he could recognize the other as Leo Fogle. Leo lived alone in a house converted out of the other and smaller feed store, noticeably smaller than its neighbours. They were not acquainted but Tim had sometimes seen the gaunt figure striding to

or from the shops, the pub or the nearest bus stop. Fogle
had a very old car which was usually to be seen in a lean-
to carport beside his house. He kept it in good running
order by dint of considerable personal labour, using parts
from one or other of the local scrap yards, but he was
more often to be seen on foot or using the local bus service.
As far as was generally known, he had no job.

In the half-light of dusk or dawn a pale dog may shine
like a beacon, a black dog can also stand out but, depending
on the light, a grey or brown dog may fade into obscurity.
As the two men converged it seemed that Umber materi-
alized from nothingness. Leo seemed startled. He recoiled
a pace.

'It's all right,' Tim said. 'She's everybody's friend.'

Leo seemed reassured but remained aloof. 'Is this the
dog that barks in the night?'

Tim felt his hackles rise. Criticism of his dog was criticism of himself. 'It's her job to bark when strangers are
around,' he said. 'That's one of the things that dogs are
for.'

Umber was staying tight to heel. Leo, aware that he
had offended a neighbour, felt the need to make amends.
'Good training,' he remarked. 'Er – I'm Leo Fogle.'

The ice had been broken at last so that, despite his
shyness, Tim felt obliged to interact. 'Thank you. I'm
Tim Russell.' They hesitated and then shook hands. Tim
was sure that for once he had encountered someone as
retiring as himself but that still did not constitute a bond.
He glanced up. The sky was brightening into an even
blue. 'I think it'll turn fine,' he said, 'I often walk the
dog about now. It's the best time of the day for thinking
out what I'm going to write.'

'I've seen you sometimes,' Fogle said. He dug into the
bulging pockets of his well-worn tweed coat and produced
a crumpled cigarette packet and a lighter. In the growing
light Tim noticed that he was singularly scruffy and that
his hands, as he lit a cigarette, were shaky. 'And I've
read one of your novels.' This, Tim decided, was about

as uninformative as you could get. As if aware that he was coming across as secretive, Fogle said, 'I'll tell you something. When I came round the corner there was somebody just here. It looked like a girl but a very odd one. Scruffily dressed and even in the poor light I could see that she looked sort of grubby. Not the sort of neighbour that we want around here. When she saw me she turned back towards the farm. She could be our burglar. Where could she be from?'

This, Tim thought, was definitely a case of the pot calling the kettle black. Fogle's fingers were stained yellow with nicotine and his nails were black-rimmed. 'I've no idea,' Tim said. 'You could always mention her to the police and see how they react.'

'I don't think I'll bother.'

Tim made some meaningless comment and they parted company. Fogle turned in to the gate of his house while Tim climbed a tubular gate and Umber slipped beneath it. The path that they were following was also the way presumably taken by the girl. Fogle was a particularly unattractive man, Tim thought, and he did not look a stud, but he was probably returning from someone's warm bed to his own.

Tim had enough to think about. The characters in his current novel had decided, as is the habit of fictitious persons, that they knew better than their creator and were acting in a fashion quite unfitted to the plot. He put Fogle out of his mind while he thought about it. He decided to introduce a third character to distract them from each other, a function for which Fogle would be totally unsuited, and then returned his attention to Umber. A canvas dummy was thrown out onto the stubble and they walked on for a hundred paces. When Umber was sent back, the dummy was retrieved perfectly and delivered sitting. It was good to start the day with a glow of satisfaction.

The path that they were following had originally been the farm track between the farm buildings and the former

feed stores. The growth of the village and the construc-
tion of a new road had forced further changes. The path
ran alongside a gulley where once a burn had tumbled
and frolicked. The burn had been reduced to a shadow
of its former self when the parent stream had been
dammed a mile away to form a reservoir and to prevent
flooding in that part of the town. The route of the burn
was marked by the trees that had seeded themselves along
its course. Among the ever-present silver birches and the
much older pines were examples of a different tree that
Tim had never bothered to identify; but these trees grew
in a dome-shaped form quite distinct from the others.
Beyond the burn was a dense spruce plantation and across
the track was a large field of pasture that Tim was treating
as out of bounds until a large covey of partridges had
flown. Meantime, he was teaching Umber that the sheep
in that field were figments of the bitch's imagination and
always to be ignored.

The gulley took a sudden bend away from the track
and left behind the cultivated area of the farm. The sun
was up and the edge of the town had receded into the
distance when Tim felt a nudge at the back of his knee.
He glanced down. One of the dome-shaped trees, about
halfway down the side of the gulley, seemed to be holding
Umber's interest but, sensing his attention, she looked up
at him and if a Labrador could be said to have eyebrows
she raised them.

The relationship between man and dog had been developing until they were now adept at reading each other's
body language – the apparently telepathic relationship
that can develop between handler and dog. He made a
gesture with one finger that released her from 'heel'. She
bounded down the slope towards the tree and then stood
stock still except for a gentle movement of her tail. After
a few seconds, reassured, she moved forward into the
dark interior of the foliage. Tim heard a voice that was
stilled as he approached rather more cautiously. There
was a distinct path down the slope and signs that, at the

steepest point, rough steps had been dug or kicked into the bank.

He ducked into the dim interior. The figure squatting on a bed of pine fronds was easily recognizable as the girl 'scruffily dressed and sort of grubby' described by Fogle. She was wearing a wrinkled khaki mackintosh over jeans and a sweater, with trainers, that had once been white, on her feet. Her hair, which was dusky blonde, had been roughly combed out and then left to look after itself. His first impression had been that she was a child bunking off from school, but a closer look suggested that she was adolescent or even a young adult. She maintained an unusual dignity for one so young.

She might have been a young relative of the farmer, camping out for fun and with permission, but the defiance in her attitude dispelled that idea. She settled on attack as being the best defence. 'You could have knocked,' she said.

'It's not so easy to knock on twigs and leaves.'

She raised her pert nose even higher. 'Suppose I'd been undressed?'

'Unlikely, in this cool weather, and unwise in the countryside, but I'm sure that I'd have considered you beautiful.'

She hesitated and then frowned. 'I don't like being towered over,' she said petulantly. 'Either sit down or go away.'

He seated himself on a wooden box. Day had broken and he saw that the space within the gloom of the tree was as well organized as any campsite that he had ever seen. Boxes and cardboard cartons on pallets around the trunk of the tree held carefully arranged possessions, tools and a sleeping bag. A sheet of polythene was folded and weighted down but ready to be used as protection. A single gas ring stood on a square of bricks, with a gas cylinder nearby. A puff of breeze rattled the leaves and she pulled up the collar of her coat.

'What are you going to do about me?' she asked suddenly.

Her hand, as if without conscious intent, was still fondling Umber's ear just where she liked it. The bitch was groaning with pleasure. He felt a twinge of jealousy.

So the girl was there without the farmer's knowledge. She was small, slim and blessed with an innocent face. Looking at her as a possible criminal hiding from the law she presented an unlikely picture but you never knew.

'I don't have to do anything about you. How long have you been living rough?' he asked.

'A few weeks,' she replied. And then, quickly, 'Why do you want to know? I'm not bothering anybody. Nobody ever comes this way.'

There might be substance here to give a fresh twist to his story. She might even represent the new character. 'This Indian summer won't last for ever,' he said. 'What will you do when it turns really cold?'

She seemed to deflate. Her defensiveness drained away. 'I don't know,' she said.

'You're not our local burglar, are you?'

She turned pink and then recovered. 'No, of course not. Do you have a local burglar? Taking big things?'

'Not usually. He seems to go in for the small and valuable plus food and drink. Look, I'm nothing to do with the police or any of the authorities,' he said gently. 'I'm just a friendly neighbour. If it's what you really and truly want, I'll go away and forget about you. But I may be able to help. Tell me how it came about.'

'Well . . .' she said. There was a long pause. 'Well, I suppose it's hardly a secret, or at least it wasn't going to stay a secret for ever. I may as well tell you, but you won't be able to help me. You won't want to.'

'You can't be sure of that. I'm the eternal boy scout.' He settled down to listen. Tim was only just out of his twenties, having made a very early start to his career. He adjusted his mind to where he thought hers would be pitched.

THREE

'I don't know where to begin,' she said, 'so I'll do it the way Lewis Carroll said. "Begin at the beginning, go on until you reach the end: then stop." It sounds simple but not many people manage it.

'I was born in this town,' she went on. 'I don't know anywhere else. That's the only reason I'm still here.' She was speaking clumsily, as if she had used her voice very little recently, but her accent was good and she articulated clearly.

'My father was the sales manager for a big wholesaler, covering a large area. It meant a lot of driving around.' She sighed. 'That's what killed him in the end – wet conditions and a foggy day, that's what the policeman said. Even so it wasn't his fault, it was the other driver going too fast, skidding and hitting him head on.'

Tim was nearly distracted by the echo of the accident that had limited his own activities and thus kick-started his career. 'One moment,' he said. 'This sounds like Walter Erskine. Was he your father? I remember when he was killed.'

She brightened. 'Yes. You knew him, didn't you? I think I saw you at his funeral. I don't know why I should remember you but I do, and hardly anyone else.'

He felt mildly flattered. Memories were flooding back. 'We used to meet in the club almost every week, have a drink or two and play snooker. We went fishing sometimes. We got on well. I think I liked him better than any other man I know. He was full of humour but it wasn't only that his humour meshed with mine. Many people can relay a joke and make people laugh but your father's humour was often original and unique. It came from the soul, if I can put it like that. I mean, he was a man who was deeply amused by life and everything embraced by it. That's all too rare. People take life too seriously. And he wasn't only a humorist. He was always a source of invaluable advice and he was an enormous help after my leg was damaged in a motorbike smash.'

She glanced down at his feet. 'I didn't know about that. What happened?'

'Much like what happened to your father, only I got away with it. A lorry skidded on wet leaves. I almost escaped it but my left foot was caught under a wheel. I lost my foot and a bit of my leg. My bike was a write-off and I spent months in hospital and learning to walk again. Your balance gets changed completely. Your father helped me a lot.'

'How did he do that?'

'Obviously I had to forget about taking a serious part in sport. A lot of things became impossible except in a bumbling and amateur sort of way. But your father helped me to see that other things were still well on the cards. We went through all the possibilities and impossibilities until we narrowed it down to the things I could do and the one that I fancied and thought that I might have a knack for was writing. Then he kept on at me until I tried my hand at it.

'My first attempt was like running through treacle but it got easier and I've been earning my living that way ever since. But we were talking about you. I used to see your mother around sometimes but I never met her.'

Her smile faded again. 'I wish . . . I wish I could say that that was your loss but I can't,' she said. 'I know it sounds awful to say such things about your own mother, but even when Dad was alive, in fact almost as far back as my memory goes, I knew that she was a long way from being the brightest fairy light on the tree. I know that he loved her in his way but sometimes, when he didn't know that I was looking, he used to cast his eyes up, the way you do when your patience is being stretched beyond all reason. From something he said once, I think that when he married her he thought that he could teach her to think for herself. But even I could see that she found it less effort to ask a silly question than to work the answer out for herself even when she knew that the answer was under her nose. You know what I mean?'

Tim knew exactly what she meant. He had known others just the same but he had no desire to get bogged down in a discussion of human stupidity and mental laziness. 'So you're Walter's daughter. He told me a little about you. Edith, isn't it?'

She pursed her lips for a moment. 'That was an extra piece of silliness on Mum's part. She insisted on naming me after an aunt of hers. She hoped that my great-aunt would leave some money or something to her namesake but it never happened. Edith, I ask you! And then she went and called me Edie where the girls at school could hear, and they started calling me Amin after you know who, and I had to pretend to like it. If we get to know each other . . .' She broke off.

'Let's assume that we will,' Tim said. He was rather attracted to this unusual person. He had still not had a very good look at her. The gently moving shadows of the leaves obscured her features, but her voice and her mind both seemed bright and cheerful. All the same, he was not sure that he would welcome any newcomers into his settled life except perhaps as characters in his fiction.

'Yes, let's. Well, would you mind calling me Ann? That's my middle name and I like it a whole lot better. I must say that boys have a much better choice of names than girls.'

He thought about it. He always found that selecting names for characters was more difficult than it might seem. 'I think that it's the other way round,' he said. 'The Americans are much more flexible with first names than we are, but it seems to me that you can call a girl absolutely anything but in this country a boy called something unusual would have the mickey taken out of him. My name's Tim. Short for Timothy.'

'Tim.' She rolled it round her tongue. 'Yes, that's a good sort of name.'

'It makes me think of the speaking clock.'

She gave a little snort of amusement. Then all the laughter went out of her face. 'But I was telling you. I don't know why I'm telling you all this, except perhaps that I've been starved of the sound of my own voice. Aren't you bored?'

'Not a bit.'

'If you say so. Well, after Dad was killed Mum was lost. He'd always done her thinking for her. He hadn't seemed to mind – at least that way he knew what she was thinking. Left on her own, her mind went blanker than ever. I tried to help her but she was too used to thinking of me as her baby. Instead, she started consulting the manager of the Spar shop, Mr Hooper.'

Tim was surprised to discover how many of the people in her life were known to him although she had never, as far as he could remember, crossed his path before. He had been a resident in the town for ten years, had belonged to one or two clubs and frequented several gathering places, but not always places where a young girl would be welcomed. On the whole he had lived a retiring life. 'Would that have been the thin man with the red hair?'

'No, he came later,' she said. 'Mr Hooper was the tall man with a bushy, black moustache.'

'And the deep gravely voice? I remember him too.'

'So do I,' she said distastefully. 'He certainly saw Mum coming – I thought she looked a thousand years old but everybody always said how young she looked. And she had her own house and a little money. So he moved in with her and they got married. They were quite good to me when they remembered – I don't think she'd have stood for any actual mistreatment of me – and it isn't as if they had a lot of rows or something, but they stopped being sloppy around each other and then along came the new minister at the Auld Kirk. That was the thin man with red hair.'

She was filling in gaps in the story of the town. This

was becoming more and more interesting. So also was her calm and unemotional statement of the facts. 'I suppose he was even more willing to do her thinking for her?'

She nodded sadly. 'Ministers do tend to be like that. Mum suddenly believed in the word of God, as told by the Reverend Mr Downing. In the end, they went off together.'

'I remember that he left under a cloud but they hushed up the reasons. Did she take you along or leave you in the care of your stepfather?'

'If she thought about it at all, she probably thought that Mr Hooper would take me on board.' Her voice cracked. Her face suddenly screwed up as though tears were on the way but she blinked violently. Tim thought that she was forcing herself to think of something bland to hold the tears back. When she had her voice under control she went on. 'He wasn't at all angry at her for going. You see, she'd left him in control of the house and things. He never spoke to me at all, which I was glad of. He moved out – he already had a flat of his own over the shop. I got by. I had copies of Mum's credit cards so at least I could buy food for the time being. In a way it was quite a happy time. But then I found that he'd been selling the house back to the housing association who'd built the house in the first place and still held what was left of the mortgage. And bills were piling up.

'I went to the council, asking for help. First of all I was sent to a man who told me that the council tax was overdue, which wasn't within a mile of being the point. Then I got passed from person to person with everybody seeming to quibble and look for reasons why I was some-body else's responsibility. They kept asking questions and starting to fill up forms and I didn't even understand the questions let alone know the answers, and some of them seemed to think I was daft and others thought I was some sort of confidence trickster, and they wanted proof of my identity which I didn't have because Mum had just shovelled everything into her bag and my birth certificate must have been in there, and the building society was saying that I'd have to be out by a date that was coming close.'

'What on earth did you do?' Tim asked. He had become so caught up in her story that the answer to his question had passed him by although he already knew it.

At their first encounter the girl had seemed remarkably controlled and in command of whatever occurred; but now her face seemed about to crumple again and he thought that she was choking back a sob. He decided that she had stayed cool by pretending to herself that her problems were unreal or were happening to somebody else. She turned away and when she spoke again it was in the loud whisper sometimes adopted when the speaker is too moved to trust their voice. 'I thought there was nothing I could do. Then I thought that was stupid. They couldn't stop me being somewhere and I might not have a lot of choice where that would be but among the very few places open to me the decision which place to choose was mine. If there were better choices I could have made I couldn't think of them.

'I put aside everything I was sure I would need again and then I got that second-hand dealer from near the bottom of Market Street to come and put a price on the rest.'

'Waller? They call him Woodworm Waller, I'm told,' said Tim, 'because it doesn't take more than an hour or two for any furniture he takes in to become infested. Did you get paid for it?'

The tears dried up and he saw her fists clench. 'A hundred and twenty miserable pounds. And there was a nearly new thirty-inch colour telly, a fridge and freezer, four beds and all the bedding . . . Oh, I could go on and on. The sitting room carpet was less than a year old and it had cost the earth. But what could I do? I had nowhere to store the stuff and nowhere to live. I stayed on for a few more days, sleeping in my sleeping bag on the floor, until I was thrown out; but I'd decided to come here and just survive until I could think of something else, so I was coming here after dark with as much as I could carry each time. I bought and brought along some tinned food but I've still got most of it left because the fields are full of food. I don't think anybody's noticed that I've taken some potatoes and a few carrots and other vegetables. And, years ago, my dad showed me how to tickle trout. Last week I spotted a hare curled down in its form but I pretended not to notice it and to walk past without looking at it. Then I made a sudden grab and snatched it up and I broke its neck just the way he'd taught me with a rabbit. It gave me meat for the whole week.'

'I give you full marks for self-reliance.' Tim gave silent consideration to what she had told him. There was no denying the truth of her story. Much of the evidence was before him, he knew some of the characters and there was no guile to be seen in her manner. 'You know that we have a burglar around here?' he asked.

She jumped as though he had stuck a needle into her. Umber, whose ear she was stroking also jumped and gave her a reproachful look. 'You just said so. Lord's sake,' she said, 'that isn't me.'

He hid his amusement rather than hurt her feelings. 'I know it isn't. It's been going on too long. But our burglar isn't an opportunist daytime thief. He seems to pick on houses with unmown front lawns or milk and paper deliveries cancelled. But if there's a house that attracts him that's never empty, he's quite prepared to emulate Flannelfoot and go in at night, moving very quietly. If you've been living a nocturnal lifestyle, you might have seen him – or her, just possibly.'

She laughed in her turn. 'I should have known that you only meant that. No, I don't think I've seen him – or her. A figure seen in the distance, perhaps, but not to recognize or remember.'

'The question was worth asking.' The question and its reply had given him time to arrive at an almost intuitive decision. 'Anyway, you can't go on living here indefinitely. As I said, winter will be here all too soon.' He pointed to the improvised cooker. 'Where will you get gas supplies from?'

She pinched her lips together – very pretty lips they were – and shook her head.

'Then I'll just have to guess. There's a caravan park just over the hill. My guess would be that you'd pinched a cylinder from there.'

She flinched again. 'I wouldn't do that. I've been going to the caravan place at night, about once a week, and swapping a half full cylinder for a three-quarters full one. And all right, I know that was less than honest but the man wouldn't sell me full cylinders and my money wouldn't have lasted long if he had.'

'Those blue cylinders can freeze,' he said. 'What do you do for water?'

'There's a stream.'

'Some of the town's water used to come from there. Then there was a scare about cryptosporidium, which can be rather nasty if you get it. What were you going to do when you needed dentistry or a doctor?'

She shrugged and looked away. 'I don't know.'

He could see problems queuing up to confront her, not all of them susceptible to solution in her simple and direct manner. The decision that he had made seemed, in retrospect, to have been inevitable. Setting aside any hypothetical obligation that he might have to a late, close friend, he had had a choice to make. The determining factor might be duration. An unknown period of disruption, expense, possibly scandal and argument against a possible lifetime of self-recrimination after the girl was raped or murdered or died a lingering death from one of the many diseases that lay in wait for those who abandoned the protection of ordered society.

'How old are you?' he asked.

'I'll be eighteen in March. Why do you want to know?'

'Because if you had been a little younger you would have been the responsibility of the local authority and I would have had no right to offer you help. As it is, I can put a roof over your head, for a while, and some food in front of you. And,' he added quickly, 'you needn't look at me like that. I'm not looking for anything in return except occasional companionship in front of the television, perhaps a little help with the chores and dog-walking and the knowledge that I'd saved my old friend's daughter from something bad.'

'Like what?'

'If I knew what, I could do something about it without disrupting my life. But something bad does await the young girl who steps outside the protection of society. To be fair, you haven't exactly stepped outside it so much as been pushed.'

'I can look after myself,' she said in a very small voice.

'You've managed to look after yourself so far. You've been brave and lucky and a little bit clever. But not everybody can be trusted. It's up to you to make up your own mind whether you can trust me. You could have my spare bedroom to yourself and I would never even look inside it except to see that you were keeping it clean and not too untidy. You can have some cupboard or garage space to store your treasures.'

Still with one arm around Umber, she looked at him appraisingly. If he knew what she was looking for he could have tried to offer it. 'I think I'll trust you,' she said at last.

'You'll have to do more than think.' He stood up, stiffly. 'I'm going home now. You can come now or later. When you walk the short way towards the town you see the backs of three houses looking at you. I live in the middle one. Knock on my door at any time.'

'Wait,' she said urgently, scrambling to her feet. 'Don't walk too quickly. I'm coming after you. I'd love a warm bath and a chance to wash my clothes properly.'

She was a scarecrow figure but most of his neighbours

would be at work or at the shops. And he had never cared very much what other people might think of him. A life spent pandering to the opinions of neighbours who he hardly knew, he thought, would have little room in it for anything creative and would soon be forgotten.

FOUR

Tim climbed back onto what there was of a path, made by deer and followed ever since by rabbits, foxes and badgers. He began to walk slowly towards home.

The girl, Ann, soon overtook him. Umber greeted her as a long-lost friend. Tim realized that the light dappling down through the leaves had not allowed him a clear view of his new companion. She was undeniably grubby. She seemed to have made an effort in the direction of cleanliness but to have been defeated by the lack of hot tap water. Her skin, however, had not suffered and he was relieved to see that she had not broken out in spots. Her mackintosh had seen better days. He wondered what she would have done when her clothes wore out. The answer would probably have been a raid on the neighbourhood's clothes-lines but it was too early to ask such a question – she seemed to be sensitive on the subject of honesty which, as he remembered her father, was not surprising. Under the unkempt surface she showed a good bone structure, delicate features and a figure, not wholly concealed by the threadbare mackintosh, which had been honed by a Spartan lifestyle into shapely slimness. Her trainers were discoloured but an effort had been made to scrub them clean. Her shoulder length hair, which seemed to be about the colour of heather honey, had been washed within the previous few days. It had been carefully brushed but the curl had returned as it dried.

Refusing his offer of help, she was carrying a cardboard carton into which she had stuffed her immediate necessities, some personal treasures and a sleeping bag. Despite this burden, she walked lightly and as she walked she jingled; otherwise there was silence between them at first. At the sight of a distant figure on a tractor she deviated from their path and walked a parallel track, out of sight below the lip of the gulley. It was clear that her time in the wild had taught her the layout of every piece of 'dead' ground where she could pass unobserved. Umber, who had been walking at heel between the pair of them, appeared nonplussed.

Tim might not put a high value on other peoples' opinions of him, but he had felt a slight concern about arriving at his own front door in such scruffy but obviously young and female company. Edith – or Ann as he had agreed to call her – had the same concern. She hesitated near the garden walls. 'You go on in and unlock your back door,' she said. 'I'm not fit to be seen like this by your neighbours.'

The garden walls were at least chest high. Rather than argue, he took the cardboard carton from her and left her to get on with it. Sure enough, when he opened the back door she was waiting on the doorstep, looking a little more ruffled than ever. She recovered her carton of treasures. 'Is it all right if I take a bath?'

They were, for the moment, out of the breeze and he was reminded that her lifestyle, without ready access to soap, hot water or paper, had not lent itself to personal freshness. But at least her upbringing was impelling her in the right direction. He was tempted to say that bathing would not only be all right, it would be obligatory, but that would have set them off on the wrong foot. 'No problem. Help yourself to whatever you need.'

He showed her the bathroom and the spare bedroom, formerly Cecily's, gave her a bath towel and what he had in the way of shampoos and leftover bubble bath. As an afterthought, he added a towelling bathrobe that he had ordered on Cecily's behalf but which had arrived after her departure. He had half intended to do some tidying in the garden but while he had few doubts about her honesty his experience of young girls was that they were inclined towards careless or malicious interference, so that it would have been against his instinct to leave a strange one of them alone in his house. He sat down instead at his word processor. Umber settled as usual with her head on his feet. As Tim tried to arrange his thoughts he heard water running in his bathroom. He had never been so attuned to the domestic noises of another person. He heard the drone of the hairdryer, which he had bought for Cecily's use but which she had left in her room. Then he heard his washing machine start up. After the spin cycle there was a long pause during which he became lost in his work. When he looked at his watch he saw that the morning had flown.

Tim was a competent cook with cordon bleu aspirations, but while living alone it had never seemed worth the bother of preparing culinary delights for a single diner and, like many a bachelor, he had become habituated to convenience foods. From the kitchen window he saw her hanging laundry on his rotary line. He took out a shepherd's pie and put it to thaw in the microwave. The text on the packaging was not specific on the subject but he guessed, from experience with an earlier clone, that it had been intended as a meal for two small persons or one giant. He prepared some extra vegetables and laid the kitchen table. When the time specified on the wrapping had expired he called up the stairs to say that lunch was ready.

Ann arrived at the kitchen door wrapped in the dressing gown, which had proved to be generous in size. The sleeves were turned up. Her hair, now blow-dried, was a paler shade of blonde and distinctly curly but it had been carefully brushed out. If she wore any make-up he could not detect it but the towelling gown emphasized her probable nudity underneath it more than mere underwear would have done and she still made a picture fit for a calendar. She pulled the gown more tightly around herself. 'You don't mind . . .?'

'The dressing gown? No, of course not. I can't think what else you would have done.' He held his mind firmly away from speculation. 'Is the room all right?'

'It's beautiful. G R Eight.' She folded neatly into the chair that he indicated. 'How are you going to explain me? Or are you planning to get rid of me quickly?'

'I hadn't given thought to either of your questions. If anybody seems curious, tell the truth and I'll do the same. You're the daughter of a late friend and you've been left in the lurch. I'm helping out. Oh, and while you're here, one little favour. Don't use text speak. As a writer I need to keep my language clear.'

She looked at him thoughtfully and then nodded. 'I'll remember. And another favour in return. I wouldn't want to be referred to as your niece,' she said.

The reminder that this was how an older man might refer to a young mistress stopped him with a jerk. He would soon have to clarify his position but for the moment a change of subject seemed to be called for. 'You washed your clothes.'

'They're on your washing line now – will that make a problem? – and I'll use your tumble-dryer if that's all right.'

'No problem,' he said. 'But you'll need some better clothes and I can't see you shopping for them if what you've got is all as ragged as what I've seen so far.'

'Couldn't you shop for me?'

He suppressed a shudder. 'No I could not.'

'Well, I'm not proud.'

Tim did not consider himself proud but if she stayed in his house for more than a day or so the news would soon circulate around the comparatively small community. He was not averse to getting a reputation for having a young and, now that he came to have a good look at her, distinctly nubile mistress, but he would not wish that person to be seen as too much of a fright. 'Can you use a needle? More to the point, can you use an electric sewing machine?'

She had tackled her meal hungrily but she paused to empty her mouth. 'Either of those. I can cook, too. My school was red-hot on domestic things.'

'I had a lady staying here,' he said, wondering as he spoke whether Cecily really qualified as a lady. He had taken her in as a night-time comfort, nothing more. 'When she left she said something about some clothes that didn't suit her and that she was leaving behind. Typical of her, I suppose, to leave me the bother of disposing of her cast-offs. Anyway I never bothered and there are still some dresses and things in the wardrobe. If you can alter any of them to fit you and turn them into something you wouldn't be ashamed to be seen in, you'd be welcome to them.'

For the moment she was more interested in satisfying her hunger. Clearly she had not seen food other than the gleanings of the farmland for some weeks. When she had cleared her plate, taken a generous portion of oatcakes with cheese and followed with two mugs of coffee, she insisted on tackling the washing up, tidying the kitchen and wiping over the working surfaces while he sat and enjoyed the luxury of having somebody else do his chores. Then at last she said, 'Shall we have a look at those clothes?'

'You don't need me.'

'I do, you know. I know a little about fashion and the design of clothes but I'm not clever with colours. I've no clue at all what looks right for my age group. And I'll need somebody to pin things.'

This all sounded quite terrifying and he was tempted to fetch one of the neighbourhood wives, but he hoped to present a tidier image of her to the world and so he decided to postpone that decision. He followed her up the stairs and into the second bedroom. Umber, filled with curiosity at these changes to routine, padded along behind. In the wardrobe there remained several good dresses on hangers and a few others, obviously considered of no account, tumbled on the wardrobe floor. Ann took them out one by one and held them up against herself while muttering comments. 'She must have been a giraffe . . . more for a garden party . . . my colouring . . .'

From the wardrobe floor she plucked up a printed cotton summer frock in pastel colours with a yellow background. Tim remembered it being worn once and then discarded. Ann said, 'This looks more like me, I'll try it on. Do you have any pins?' Tim recalled a pincushion, once belonging to some female relative, which he had last seen in the drawer of the dressing table.

When he returned his attention to the room he was stunned. She had removed both the jeans and blouse that she had been wearing, each showing serious wear and tear, and stood before the wardrobe mirror in small and severely plain pants. Her back was to him but in the mirror he could see that her young breasts were sweetly rounded. She had no bra; indeed, she had no great need of one although he had glimpsed several on the washing line. Her figure flowed from curve to curve so prettily that he was dumbstruck. He thought that he had seen beauty, indeed he had become lyrical in his writings on such sights as landscape, flowers, horses, girls and cloud-scapes, but now he recognized real beauty for the first time. Then the dress dropped like a stage curtain, extinguishing the sight, and something had gone out of the day.

She turned to face the room. 'You're blushing,' she said. 'Shouldn't I have done that? Nobody ever complained before.'

He just stopped himself from saying 'I'll bet'. Instead he took a seat on the dressing-table stool and said huskily, 'You must remember that in a few short years, perhaps since your mother moved out, you've gone from a girl to a young woman. But I'm not complaining. You're very beautiful.'

It was her turn to blush. She opened her mouth – such a tender mouth had surely been created for kissing – but closed it again without speaking. The dress hung loosely on her. She directed him as he began, very carefully, to put in pins at the shoulders, the hem, round the waist and down the seams until they could both see how it could look. 'The neckline isn't quite right,' she said. 'It takes too much of a dip. If you're very critical you'll be able to see that the dress has been made down from somebody bigger, but this is as good as we can get it without remaking the whole collar and it's quite good enough to go shopping for new jeans in.'

'And to go and see your friend Mr Waller.'

She said, 'What?' and she looked afraid.

'You can't have much money left.'

'I haven't. About forty quid.'

'And when that's gone, will you be happy to have to come and ask me for pocket money and a clothes allowance? We'd both want you to feel that what you had would be truly your own. I knew your father so I feel that I know you, but you only met me today.'

She looked down at the floor. 'I hadn't thought so far ahead. But I can quite see that it wouldn't be fair to you.'

Tim was aware of being pulled in several directions. He could not deny, even to himself, that the departure of Cecily had left a gap in his comfort. He was still in the prime of life with all his male instincts in full flow and his sleep had sometimes been disturbed by fantasies very similar to the vision that he had just seen. But he told himself sternly that her youth, her apparent innocence, his friendship with her father and the assurance that he had given her all precluded him from making sexual advances. But he could still help her, ease her return into society. With the sight of her nakedness fresh in his memory, along with the vision of her confronting him in the untidily pinned dress, he wanted to tell her that she would be more than welcome to pocket money and a clothing allowance, that he would like to dress her from the skin out in the best and finest without thought of any favours in return, but he lost his nerve. It was too soon, much too soon.

'Don't think of it that way,' he said. 'You're a little past the age for being adopted, but I'm not too short of money. If I'd had a daughter I could have looked after her. For the moment, you can take her place; but we have to think what's to become of you. We'll talk about it again.'

His erection had subsided. His electric sewing machine must have been one of the first ones made. It had been bought for a song and seldom used, but the action was heavy and sounded good, with a Rolls Royce sort of solidity. He fetched it from the attic – she had to help him to steady it on the loft ladder. He had a box of coloured threads saved for fly-tying. Ann soon had the machine working away, sewing a perfect line. When he was satisfied that she had all that she needed he went back to his word processor.

His mind had clarified and the plot had shaken out into coherence and artistic balance, without much conscious input from him. He could see the convolutions of the stresses between the characters stretching into the distance.

This one was going to be good. He settled to work and soon reality had melted away and he was living entirely within his own dreamworld, existing as each character in turn.

FIVE

Tim was fetched out of his trance-like state by Ann, but only to attend to her announcement, in the light of her claim to have learned cookery at school and in her anxiety to please, that she would cook the evening meal. Tim had already carried his day's work to the point of exhaustion so he found himself unexpectedly free to make an extra visit to the gym.

With a skill that, for no good reason, he found surprising, Ann had remade the seams of the yellow dress and after putting it on for Tim's approval she intended to wash the finished article and hang it to dry; but it would not be wearable until next day when she also planned to start work on a cream tennis dress. Tim found an aerosol of ivory cellulose in his garage, left over from a car long since traded in, and the trainers were given a respray. Although the low heels did not flatter the ensemble, she was not short in the leg and she began to look very much more like a finishing school graduate and less like the Artful Dodger.

While Tim took Umber to the gym and back for her evening walk rather earlier than usual (leaving the bitch sitting steadfastly outside the door), Ann cooked with an apron over the towelling dressing gown that Tim was beginning to see as part of her image. When he returned he had half expected her to have vanished, either as an ephemera of his imagining or because she had thought better of walking into his parlour, but she was still there and at work. In the bottom of the freezer she had found a pair of pork fillets that he had quite forgotten and though she was working without some of the ingredients that she considered necessary, she managed to produce a very creditable feast. Tim, who rarely drank except in the pub, opened a bottle of good, white Bordeaux that he had been saving for a special occasion.

Ann startled him by saying, 'It should really be a red. Or a rosé.'

'Who taught you about wines?'

'My dad. He wanted me to know everything. He never stopped teaching me things, he said that nobody could ever know too much. He started me reading. Do you mind if I borrow some of your books?'

'Help yourself. But my last lady friend took away a lot of my favourites.' He looked at her curiously. Personal questions seemed to be acceptable. 'I've been listening to you. I'm a writer, as you know. You seem to have the usual limited use of words that young girls seem satisfied with these days, but if you're a reader I'd have expected a wider vocabulary.'

She grinned at him, creating a whole new image. Suddenly she was mischievous and at the same time knowing. 'My dad told me never to use a long word if a short one would do. He said that using long words was a way of showing off. But I'm perfectly capable of grandiloquence or even circumlocution if the situation justifies it.'

'Your father was quite right,' he said. They laughed together for the first time and then settled down to enjoy a good meal in an atmosphere that was almost festive.

'The wine is white,' Tim said, 'because red wine very rarely crosses my doorstep. I'm a martyr to gout but it only seems to happen if I drink red wine. It's the purines that do it. Yes, I know that I have only one foot to have gout in, perhaps that's why it's especially bad when I get it. It's very unpleasant and painful and I'd rather not have it again.'

It was Tim's habit after his evening meal, if Umber had been walked and he had no outside engagements, to settle down to read or watch television. As soon as she had pried this information out of him, Ann coaxed him into continuing that pattern while she cleared the kitchen and then, with dusk approaching, resumed some of her ragamuffin clothes while she slipped out to bring the remainder of her possessions from her former bivouac to storage in the garage. Umber stayed with her master.

Tim had settled in front of a documentary about ancient history but it failed to hold his attention and, anyway, he disagreed with many of its conclusions. Instead of watching it, he was asking himself a swarm of questions. Where, if anywhere, was this relationship going? Where did he want it to go? Why was he laying himself open to disaster of one kind or another? Duty to an old friend or attraction in one of its many forms? How was he going to steer their course for the coming days? What was her future to be? Was she asking herself the converse questions? Most crucial of all, how did she see him?

'Am I being an idiot?' he asked Umber. 'You like Ann, don't you?' Recognizing the name, Umber rose to her feet and looked at the door, her tail gently waving. 'She must be all right, then. Dogs are often the best judges of people.' He wondered why that was true. He made a note to think about it, perhaps to form a theme in some future book. It had become part of his philosophy that no worthy thought should ever be wasted.

Ann returned seconds later. 'I felt that I was being watched,' she said. 'Can one really feel eyes on one?'

This was a question that he had considered for an earlier book. He killed the sound on the television. 'Frankly, no. But you can think you do, if you have reason to imagine it.'

She nodded. 'That makes sense. I heard sounds among the trees that could have been made by an animal and twice I thought that I saw somebody move, but it was dusk and I couldn't be sure. A deer, seen head-on, can have much the same silhouette as a person.'

She settled in another chair, close by. They fell into conversation. She was well informed and had an open, original mind. He soon stopped seeing her as young or feminine, she was just a like-minded friend who was spending the evening in amusing discussion. She had some of her father's humour although she did not yet have the experience to give it full rein. But that would come.

Early bedding was another of his habits and Ann, who had become accustomed to sleeping while the sun slept, seemed amenable. Assuring him that she had all that she needed, she shut herself into what had become her room and soon the house was at peace. Tim lay and turned the same questions over again in his mind without arriving at a sensible answer to any one of them.

Morning did not bring any answers. He decided to go with the flow and solve each problem as it arose. She came to breakfast in the towelling dressing gown and seemed satisfied with the breakfast that he always took – cereal, toast and honey. She smelled of soap and clean girl. He thought of buying her a perfume suited to her age and nature.

'Get yourself dressed and smartened up,' he said. 'We have to start our shopping.'

'Do you need me with you?'

'Definitely.'

The trainers had been muddied again and had to be washed. 'I can wear them wet on my bare feet,' she said.

'That you can not. The first requirement is shoes and no shop is going to tolerate your wet feet in their brand new shoes.' The idea that shoes had to be tried on before purchase was obviously novel to her, which explained the calluses on her toes. She accepted the edict and the hairdryer was called into play again while Tim brought his Mini out of the garage and checked the tyres. They set off, heading for the town to which their village was a neighbour, almost a suburb. The quarter mile of road linking the two was relieved by a service road on each side and a single row of houses looking both naked and ashamed without the backing of neighbours. Beyond, farmland began again.

The first shoe shop that they visited had in the window a pair of cream, calfskin shoes that they both admired but, she said, they were beyond what she could afford. 'Try them on,' Tim said. 'If they fit you – properly, mind – buy them. That doesn't just mean if you can get them on, it means if you can get them on without hurting your toes or any rubbing. They'll be my treat.'

Ann raised her eyebrows but she complied without a word. She came out of the shop to let him satisfy himself that the shoes were a good fit. When they were in the car and moving again she said, very quietly, 'Thank you. I didn't want to be what they call a drain on your resources. How long are you going to put up with me as a parasite?'

'You're not a parasite.'

'What am I, then?'

She could have been expecting any answer from 'delightful guest' to 'potential prey'. He watched her face in the mirror as he said, 'You're my guest and the daughter of my old friend. And I don't think that you have to be more of a drain than you want to be. I'm going to try to get you what you're owed.' He pulled up at the rundown frontage of the untidy establishment of James 'Woodworm' Waller.

If her face showed anything, it was trepidation. 'I don't want to go in there,' she said.

'Why not?'

'He unsettles me.'

Until that moment he had seen her as imperturbable and remarkably brave for her age, but she had lost colour and there was a slight tremor in her lower lip. 'Hello!' he said. 'What did Woodworm say or do to get you so uptight?'

'Nothing, really. Nothing that I could put into words.'

'Try hard.'

She produced an uncertain smile while she thought about it. 'I couldn't quote a single deed or word that was openly threatening,' she said at last. 'It was just his expression, his attitude, his body language, they were

all overpowering. He had to come and see the goods at
what had been my home and of course he could see
immediately that I was being put out, so he had me at a
disadvantage and he knew it. Whenever I tried to point
out that what he was offering was less than the stuff was
worth he'd look at me as though I was dung beneath his
wheels and tell me that I was welcome to go elsewhere.
As though there was anywhere else!'

'Would you still be afraid to come in if you have me
beside you and doing the talking?'

'Well . . .'

'Would it help if I told you that I was a boxing champion not so very long ago?'

She managed a laugh. 'It might.'

'Well, consider it said. And now, "stiffen the sinews,
summon up the blood".'

She managed to summon up the smile that had pierced
him during the previous evening. 'And I'll try to "disguise
fair nature with hard-favoured rage".'

That riposte came as a surprise to him and a delightful
one. The average Scot is better read in Burns than in
Shakespeare.

'You *are* well read,' he said. 'You like Shakespeare?'

'Yes. My dad was at school in England so he knew
Shakespeare better than Burns; he introduced me.
Shakespeare's not easy to read and I've never heard his
lines spoken by anybody who sounded as though they
really understood it. It was obviously written to be spoken.
Spoken in my head, it sounds great. I think it would be
just mind-blowing to hear it performed by a good actor.'

'Some day, we'll fit in a trip to Stratford-on-Avon.
Now, are you ready?'

'Yes.'

'Then listen.' He spent some minutes in outlining the
lines that he might take and the ways in which he would
want her support if arguments took certain turns. She
followed him into the shop, which was stacked and piled
with furniture to the high ceiling so that the eye could

hardly make out its dimensions. It smelt of dust and grubby owners with a musty overtone of fungus.

There was silence but Tim sensed that somebody was listening, perhaps hoping that some remark would betray what these customers were after. He was reminded of Ann's question about the sensation of being watched. They waited quietly. There was a sudden shuffle of feet and the proprietor made his appearance. Mr Waller was a large man and very stout. His face and head were highly coloured but he was totally hairless except for several days worth of stubble on his jowls. He wore dusty dungarees and carpet slippers.

'Can I help you?'

'I'm sure you can,' Tim said, keeping his voice carefully friendly but businesslike. He produced the list that Ann had prepared at his insistence. 'We've come to collect the balance that you owe this young lady.'

Mr Waller's smile was replaced by a lordly frown. 'I never seed her afore.'

Tim looked enquiringly at her.

'He came to my house,' Ann said. 'He gave me a hundred and twenty pounds for all the furniture and what they call white goods like cooker and—'

Mr Waller decided that he did after all remember her. 'That's all it was worth,' he said with an air of finality.

Ann patted the arm of a plum-coloured leather settee that was perched on top of a dining table and supporting three mattresses. 'This was our living room suite,' she said. 'There's a price ticket on it. It says a hundred and ten pounds.'

'I wouldn't expect to get that much for it,' Mr Waller explained hastily. 'That's a starting figure, for arguing over.'

'And you've already sold the chairs?'

'Ten pound each, that's a' that I got.' From his tone of voice Tim judged that he did not expect to be believed.

'This way,' Ann said. She was regaining confidence now that she did not have to face Waller alone. She led

Tim to an offshoot of the main space, where the cream of his stock was stored. This consisted of refrigerators, freezers and other 'white goods'. She patted a large fridge-freezer. 'This was ours. The ticket says ninety-five. How much did you get for the tumble dryer, the washing machine and the dishwasher?' she demanded.

Mr Waller decided to abandon any attempt at sweet reason. 'Nane o' your bluidy business,' he snapped. 'I bocht yon goods fair an' square. Now, get out.'

Tim had been using his eyes. There was a battered bookcase against the far wall. 'And you bought these books fair and square?' he asked.

'What if I did?'

'They're mine. You'll find that each one has my book-plate in it with my phone number. So you've been buying stolen goods without even checking that the seller had the right to sell them.'

'So he's not only a swindler, he's a fence as well,' Ann said.

The dealer came to the boil. 'You'll take that back.' He stepped towards Ann but Tim, who could be quite fleet despite his disability, moved between them. Waller made to brush him aside but when Tim stood firm he balled his fist and swung a punch. Tim slipped aside and delivered his own punch to the space where the other's ribs divided. Waller sat down suddenly on the hard floor and tried to breathe, without a great deal of success. Tim pulled out a chair and placed it for Ann before stepping to the door and turning the sign to CLOSED. He stepped on Waller on the way past, each way. He took a second chair for himself and they sat quietly, watching the dealer as he struggled for breath but without offering help or comfort.

Waller managed a gasp and then dragged some air into his lungs. Tears were hopping down his plump and badly shaven cheeks and his colour paled from purple to scarlet. He began to pant like a dog and dragged himself slowly to his feet. His face left them in no doubt that he was

furiously angry and had every intention of proving it. It
seemed that nobody had ever seen fit to warn him never
to launch himself at an enemy who had already shown
himself to be fast and ruthless. Waller grabbed Tim by
the lapels with the obvious intention of pulling him up
and onto a headbutt. Tim allowed the dealer's pull to help
him to his feet but the attempted head-butt went seriously astray. The dealer's brow met Tim's hand which
had been slipped between their heads and was already
gripping his, Waller's, nose and pushing upwards. Waller
staggered back, bubbling blood down his shirt-front. He
bumped into a stack of furniture, nearly bringing a nest
of tables down on his own head.

'That's quite enough,' Tim said gently, rubbing a slight
bruise on his forehead. 'Any more violence and the young
lady will scream "Rape!" and tear her dress and I'll run
in from the street and feel free to beat the hell out of
you. I'll be the hero for saving her from actual rape, but
attempted rape is serious enough. You can be put away
for quite a long time and you'd go on the Sex Offenders
Register which would follow you around for years. Now
answer the lady's question.'

Waller was now very sorry for himself. He managed
to make hooting sounds that his listeners interpreted as
'You've broken my bloody nose.' He had also lost two
teeth.

'You broke your own nose, trying to give me a head-
butt. And if you don't answer the lady's question I'll take
hold of your nose and give you a good shaking by it.'

The dealer indicated that he had forgotten the question.

'The young lady wished to know how much you got
for those of her goods you've already resold.'

Waller looked longingly at the door but there was no
help on offer and Tim was already established in the way.
The dealer humped himself to his feet. He hesitated,
glaring, but decided that he was no match for Tim. He
fetched a large ledger which he slammed down and
opened on a badly worm-eaten side table and left for

them to study while he nursed his nose and crooned sooth-
ingly to it.

Ann soon found the items relating to her family's
chattels. After only a few seconds of study she said, 'Never
mind what he got for the stuff, it says here what he paid
me for it and there are receipts signed with my name but
a signature that looks nothing like mine. They add up to
many times more than what I actually got.'

Tim looked for himself. 'That would seem to figure,'
he said. 'He would want to minimize his profit for the
benefit of the VAT inspector and the tax man. That, of
course, is fraud. Will you settle for what he says here
that he paid you? Or do we take this book to the police?
You can bear witness that he tried to strike the first blow
each time.'

More than an hour went by before they returned to
Tim's car, carrying his books in four large carrier bags.
There was a parking ticket on the windscreen. 'Never
mind,' Anne said. She chuckled nervously. 'Have this one
on me.' She was tucking away a healthy little bundle of
grubby banknotes as she spoke.

'That phrase came a little too readily to your tongue,'
Tim said. 'Be careful how you employ it in future. Letting
your generous heart run away with you can come expensive. Just this once I won't even accept your kind but
impulsive offer.'

SIX

The first mile of their road homeward passed in silence as Ann counted the money that Mr Waller had reluctantly disgorged. She looked up with her eyes wide. 'I've never even seen so much money,' she said, 'let alone had it for myself. I should give you something for my food and heating . . . and share of the television . . . and wear and tear and—'

'Stop!' Tim said. It came out with more force than he had intended and she gaped at him. 'You can stop thinking up more and more unreasonable reasons for giving me money that I don't want and wouldn't accept anyway. Are you going to go on cooking and cleaning and bed making?'

'I think it's the least I can—'

'Stop it,' he said, more gently this time. 'What you cost me in food and all the rest is much less than I'd have to pay a daily woman. And I suppose you're going to take the garden over from me as well?' he added hopefully. He had never really accepted that the effort and boredom of gardening was justified by the ultimate results. A garden might be delightful to stroll or sit in, to smell the flowers or even more so to recline and watch somebody else hard at work, but the sweat and boredom of digging or weeding was strictly for those times when he needed to keep his hands occupied while his mind grappled with the problems of literary composition.

Ann looked doubtful. 'I don't know much about gardening but I'm sure I could learn, if you go on putting up with me.'

'My . . .' Tim pulled himself up. He had been about to address her as his dear girl, which was becoming too close to the truth for saying aloud. 'My goodness,' he substituted. 'I'm not just putting up with you. As I said, if I had to pay a daily woman to do what you do, it would cost much more than you cost me; and doing it for myself usually takes up writing time that I can't really spare, so I rush at it and do it badly, which is why you probably think, quite rightly, that the house is a mess. Believe me, you're pulling your weight – even without putting a value on the stimulus that having a pretty girl around the place gives me and my writing. And it's very helpful to hear another voice around the house. Authors of fiction shouldn't live alone or they forget the cadences and the figures of speech that people use.'

She looked round at him again and pursed her lips. 'I don't think you should call me pretty,' she said. 'I'll accept beautiful because Aristide du Pont wrote that all girls are beautiful.'

'Where did you get that from?' Tim asked her. She shrugged.

'I don't remember. I think it was on television and it stuck in my memory because I wanted it to be true.'

'It's true. I'll swear to that. But Aristide du Pont was a name used by Aristide Briand.' He found a parking space outside a large store displaying women's clothes. 'Go on in. I'll wait here.'

'What for?'

'For you to come out again.'

She aimed a playful punch at his upper arm and then waited anxiously to see whether he would take offence. Tim had to make an effort to drag his eyebrows down. From his own experience he would have expected a more positive reaction. 'You're a girl. You have money. You need clothes. Go ahead but don't go mad.'

'I've got clothes, or I will have when I've done the other alterations. I could do with a new pair of jeans, maybe two pairs, but this isn't the right sort of shop.'

'You also need underwear. What I saw on the line seemed to have been laundered the native way, by being bashed on a rock.'

'That's true,' she said gravely, 'but I've grown up since my mother bought that stuff for me. I wouldn't know what to get. I haven't been reading the fashion magazines. Will you come in with me?'

Tim was by no means unacquainted with ladies' underwear but he was a shy man. He could have enjoyed helping this nubile young woman to choose her lingerie from a catalogue, but the idea of doing so under the amused scrutiny of several female shop assistants came close to his idea of hell. Ann and he must each be known locally and he could imagine some giggling over the teacups. 'Ask the ladies in the shop to help you,' he said. 'But don't let them sell you anything too fancy. They'll be wanting the commission, but what you're looking for is the cheap and cheerful. Practical,' he amended when she looked confused. 'Comfortable, hard wearing and you'll want some warm and some cool to suit the weather.'

She nodded uncertainly but she went into the shop. Tim made a quick visit to a nearby supermarket in order to provide for a younger and greater appetite. It was half an hour before she returned, tossed a few lightweight packages onto the back seat and settled down beside him. 'You were right,' she said. 'They wanted to sell me things that were much too good to cover up but I did what I thought you meant. I'll show you later. Tell me,' she went on without giving him time to protest. 'I thought you were joking when you said you'd been a boxing champion but now I think it must have been true. Were you?'

'Only at county level. Didn't you notice the silverware on the mantelpiece?'

'Just as part of the scenery. I mean, people often have silverware but they didn't always win it themselves, usually it was left to them by an uncle or somebody. But what you did to his nose, that wasn't boxing.'

'No,' he said, 'that certainly wasn't boxing. That was one of life's dirtier tricks, but I didn't feel under any obligation to fight fair. Perhaps I'd better explain.' He had begun to drive but the story was not for telling while an important part of his mind was elsewhere. He pulled in to a vacant parking space. 'When I was young and cocky and at the height of an undistinguished boxing career, before my leg got damaged, I saw a weedy young man being picked on by three yobs. I went to his help and they turned on me. Of course he took to his heels and that's when I found out that I couldn't lick the whole world after all. After I moved here I found that Charlie, at the Mickleglen Gym, was one of the top performers in the martial arts. He was born in Japan where his father was a consular official. He used to be flown out to Japan to judge contests in judo, kung fu, karate, you name it. I only started going to him to keep up my fitness and not to forget how to box but we became good friends and he took me in hand. He taught me to defend myself against any sort of attack and I still try to get to the gym once or twice a week to keep myself fit and my reflexes sharp. Charlie said that if I was going to rush to the aid of under-dogs like a knight rushing to save a damsel in distress, I'd better know how to look after myself. He's dead now, poor Charlie. He got shot while defending himself against a mugger in Yokohama. And it turned out that he'd left his wallet in his hotel room so he might just as well have let the mugger take whatever he had on him.'

He seemed to have lost his audience. 'Wait a minute, please,' she said. He had parked outside a much more downmarket shop and she went inside. She was back in five minutes. 'There,' she said. 'That's my shopping for clothes done for the next year or more. Three jumpers, two nighties and two pairs of jeans. We can go home now if you like and make a bonfire with all my old clothes. You don't mind me calling your house home?'

He started the car. 'I like it,' he said.

'I think that's very sad about your friend Charlie, and ironic too. Were you thinking of me as a damsel in distress when you came to my aid?'

'I wasn't thinking of you that way, I just saw you as the daughter of a late and good friend who had fallen on hard times, but that's what you were. A damsel and in distress.'

'I suppose that's true. I never thought of myself as a damsel, but I suppose that's what I am; any girl would have been referred to as a damsel and I seem to fall within the definition. Are you my knight in shining armour?'

Tim found himself in some difficulty. Did he want her to think of him in the romantic and probably sexless image of the classical knight in arms, too encapsulated in armour to attempt sex? Or did the damsel usually come to think of the knight as deserving whatever he cared to take? The writer inside him came to his rescue. 'I'm not sure of the origin of *damsel*,' he said. 'Think of yourself as a maiden. That comes direct from the German *mädchen*.' The word also had another meaning as *virgin*, but that was a subject that would not be touched on yet, if ever.

She seemed determined to put him on the spot. 'But you haven't answered me,' she said. 'Are you my knight in armour?'

He retreated into pedantry. 'What do you think? There's not much call for armour these days and the old style of amour wouldn't be much protection against modern weapons. And I have never been offered a knighthood, though I live in hope. You can tell me later,' he said. He thought that he would need thicker armour if he was to resist the attacks of her unconscious sexuality.

Tim was still putting the car away when Ann dashed upstairs to change into her new jeans. This suited Tim, who wanted nothing more than to get back to his writing, but he had got no further than to start his PC booting up when she descended again and found him waiting before an unchanging screen. 'This damn thing always takes for ever,' he grumbled.

'Let me sit down,' she said. She used her bottom to bump him aside. 'I had to spend a lot of time with computers at school when I'd rather have been out of doors. Never try to get the beastly thing to do more than one thing at a time. Think of it as having a secretary inside it who's going to get hopelessly muddled if you change your mind. Give it a single instruction and wait until it's done it before touching it again. Which program do you want?' Within a few seconds she had the PC tamed and the Word program running.

He had done little more than to read over his few words from the day before when he was called to lunch. With soup, crusty bread, cheese and biscuits and fruit disposed of, he carried his coffee cup back to his desk and prepared to join in his imagination the characters as they faced the next stage of his novel, but the doorbell jerked him back into the here and now. Ann was busily washing up and his own concentration was broken so he went to the door.

Waiting on the doorstep, foot tapping impatiently, was a beetle-browed, craggy looking man who topped Tim by several inches in each direction. Tim, who counted himself as being of average size, had the advantage of standing on a step and yet he was looking the other in the eye or very little more. 'You're Mr Russell?' the man asked. Tim had an impression that the man was trying to sound friendly but that his natural voice was rough. 'Is my daughter here?'

Tim recognized the approach of trouble that had been inevitable all along. He had already decided to meet it head to head. 'Who might that be?' Tim asked.

'Edith Erskine.'

'You are not Mr Erskine. He was a friend of mine and he was killed several years ago.' Recognition was dawning on Tim. 'I know you now. Your name is Hooper and you used to have a thick moustache. You manage one of the shops. You married Walter Erskine's widow and split up with her, leaving her daughter adrift, which doesn't make you her father. Far from it.'

The other's accent thickened. 'Stepfather, then. The young lass you're shagging is my stapdauchter an ye'll no' want me makkin a stishie—'

He broke off as Tim stepped down onto the path. Glancing around, Tim was relieved to see that if any of his neighbours were at home none was outside and paying any attention. He kept his voice low just the same. 'I have never laid a finger on the girl you left in the lurch,' he said. 'I was a friend of her father and when I learned that she had been deserted by those who should have been responsible for her and was down on her luck, the least I could do was to offer her a home while she needed it.' He was becoming heated and his tongue was running away with him. 'You never gave a damn whether she was starving or living in a cardboard box or on the streets. You're the last person to have any rights in connection with Miss Erskine.'

Hooper sneered. Tim filed away a mental description of his facial expression as being exactly what he would use when next one of his characters needed to express scornful disbelief. 'And wi' oot looking for a wee bit o hochmagandie in return? She's under age and I've come tae tak her back.' Mr Hooper seemed less sure of his ground.

'You came to try a little blackmail. What does her mother say about that?'

'Leave her mither oot o' this.'

'I can quite believe that you'd like that. I'll tell you again that I've never touched the girl, but if I did it would still be none of your business. She's over the age of consent. Does her mother know that you were selling the house and leaving her daughter penniless?'

Mr Hooper's pugnacious jaw was thrust further out and he stepped closer to Tim. 'I thocht I telled you tae leave her mither oot—'

Tim was speaking softly but his voice overrode the other's. 'You're in no position to tell me a damn thing.'

Hooper balled his fists. Behind his back Ann, who had emerged from the house through the back door and hurried round the gable, was dancing to and fro silently on Tim's tiny patch of grass, with a big grin on her face, while miming an uppercut. It seemed a sensible suggestion but not one likely to be approved by neighbours defensive about property values, so when Hooper grabbed his wrists Tim broke the hold with a quick twist against the thumbs, cupped his hands and clapped the other man's ears. The shock of compressed air within his Eustachian tubes was stunning. A punch that had been aimed at Tim's face was aborted. Hooper fell to his knees and lowered his head to the paved path. He made a subdued retching noise. From a distance he might have appeared to be weeding between the slabs. Umber had rushed forward to go to her master's aid, but when she realized that no help was needed for the moment she lay down and watched the shopkeeper's face with a lifted lip from a distance of a few inches. Hooper opened his eyes but, seeing a set of white and apparently sharp teeth very close, he closed them again.

'If you ever come back here,' Tim said softly, 'I will do that again, much harder. I will also ask some nasty questions about the real ownership of the house and furniture.' Tim had done some research for a novel about a runaway girl and parts of it were rushing back at him. 'I'll tell you something else. Listen to what I'm telling you, I may ask questions later. Your stepdaughter may be past the age of consent but under Scots Law in becoming her stepfather you took on the responsibilities of a parent until she is eighteen, without gaining the powers. The responsibilities include contributing to her further education. I am planning to send her to university and I'll be chasing you for your contribution to her fees and living expenses.

'Your stepdaughter and I are now going to walk the dog. Do not be here when we come back or you will be a very sorry shopkeeper. Your treatment of her was so despicable that I am just looking for an excuse to finish what I started.'

He helped Hooper into a more comfortable and seemly position, sitting on the grass and leaning against a tub

holding a well grown lavatera; then they locked up carefully and set off with Umber onto the farmland. The lavatera,
he thought, would have to be pruned shortly. He would
show Ann how to do it. They started walking.

'Were you really going to send me to uni?' Ann asked
softly.

'Not unless you want to go. Do you have enough exam
results?'

'More than enough. I never liked playing a lot of silly
games and I thought that learning things was interesting,
so I seemed to collect exam results the way other girls
collected stamps or boyfriends. But I don't think I want
to go. What I've seen of the student's lifestyle doesn't
attract me and I'm not looking for a business career.'

'What are you looking for in life?' Tim asked before
he could stop himself.

'I don't know yet. I'll know it when I think of it.'

Tim breathed again. 'When you're sure, we'll talk
again,' he said.

Already it seemed to be assumed between them that
their relationship was permanent. That was good but if
he was being put in the position of an adopted father, he
thought, he could hardly bear it.

Umber had been carrying one of the canvas dummies
and pushing it occasionally against Tim's leg. Obtaining
no reaction, he tried Ann with better result. Recognizing
an obligation that was not going to go away, they turned
their attention to providing a series of retrieves from the
gulley.

SEVEN

The scope of Ann's help became evident next day, which was a Saturday. The day dawned clouded, damp with drizzle. Tim refused to let the clock rule his life. He always slept with the curtains drawn back so that he could assess the day. He took one look at the droplets on the window, listened for a moment and went back to sleep. He rose later than his usual and came downstairs, dressed and shaved, to find his computer already booted up and his previous day's work loaded on the screen.

Ann was in the kitchen and his breakfast was on the table. 'Did I forget to log off last night?' he asked her.

She shook her head. 'I logged on for you. I noticed that your laptop takes a long time to boot up so I set it going. It probably needs to be defragged – I could do that for you. Then, when you didn't come down, I loaded what you'd been working on last night. I hope that was all right?'

He poured milk onto his cereal. 'Just fine. Bless you.'

She looked uncomfortable. 'I read through your novel, as far as it's gone. I'd seen some of it so I thought I might just as well see the rest while I waited for you. After all, a secret isn't a secret if you know part of it. Do you mind?' She waited anxiously.

Tim's mind cringed at the thought of his work in embryo being seen by another and not very sophisticated soul. 'You know what they say about fools and children not seeing unfinished work?'

She flushed and bit her lip. 'Which am I?'

He thought that he had hurt her feelings. If it had been possible he would have liked to call the words back but it would be as well to get the house rules clear from the start. 'I don't know. Tell me what you thought of it, as far as it's gone.'

Ann was obviously startled to be asked for her opinion on his work. She had looked on Tim's words as being set in stone. She put her mind to an assessment of what she had read and to recalling her reactions as she had read it. 'I thought . . . I thought it's obviously in short form, for filling out later, which is why it reads sort of staccato. I thought that the girl's character has been changing and you'll probably want to alter it at the beginning to be more consistent and make her a bit less bossy, otherwise the bit where she goes soft and moony won't read right. And I noticed that you'd changed the colour of her eyes after the first few pages.'

Tim made a mental note about eye colours and then hurried to make amends. 'You're neither a fool nor a bairn,' he said. 'That's a very good summary. You were absolutely right, I was going to change those bits and what I need most of all is somebody who can spot those silly mistakes and make sensible suggestions. I need to be able to see my work through somebody else's eyes. I haven't had anyone like that since . . .' He nearly said *my ladyfriend before last* but bit the words off. '. . . not for ages. You're welcome to read and make comments any time. Where did you think that the plot was going to lead?'

She had flushed with pleasure. 'I'll think about it and tell you later.'

He smiled. 'That's another good answer,' he said. 'You have the next few hours to think about it. When I've finished breakfast I'm going into the garden for a while.'

'But it's wet!'

'That's when it's easiest to get all the roots of the weeds out. When the soil's dry and hard you're more likely to leave the rootlets behind to start growing into new weeds and get even more of them than before.' He sighed. 'Living next to farmland, you can't win. Weed seeds are blowing around all the time. But you have to try. Somebody should produce a book of recipes making use of ground elder, creeping buttercup and docks. Then one could let the back garden run to weeds and comfort oneself with the thought that one was really growing vegetables.'

She bubbled with laughter. 'Can't you make salad with them?'

'Some of them. Nettles have their uses. I don't know which of the others are edible or foul tasting or even poisonous. Next time we're near the public library you can take out one or two books and make some notes. We might get a book out of it.'

An hour later a pair of muddy bare feet appeared beside him. Umber stood up and wagged her whole latter end. Tim looked up. The drizzle had stopped but the day remained misty. Ann had come to join him. Below her old mackintosh her feet and lower legs were bare. 'Be careful,' he said. 'I don't think there's any broken glass in the soil, but be careful anyway. There's a smaller pair of Wellingtons in the downstairs cloaks you can have, left by the last lady to occupy your room. She wasn't a Wellington sort of person anyway.'

'I'll try them on later.'

'Take a pair of my socks to wear with them.'

She worked with him, learning the names of plants and which were to be saved or removed, which ones had to be dug out and which could be dislodged by a straight pull, and where to put them so that they could not take root again. They knocked off for lunch and she rejoined him during the afternoon, wearing the boots that had been abandoned by Cecily over a pair of Tim's socks. The day remained dark and was becoming darker when she went back indoors.

Tim worked on.

He was suddenly aware of waking up on a hard bed. He had the sort of blinding headache that would have made death a merciful release and no recollection of an interval or any cause for a hangover. Somebody was towering over him who he recognized, without identifying any visible clues, as a nurse and not tall at all. He said 'What?'

The nurse smiled reassuringly. 'Do you know who you are?'

He particularly did not want to think but the question of his identity seemed important to him. 'I know who I am. I just don't care. I think I'd rather be somebody else just now. Want to be sick.'

He was enormously sick, some of it through his nose. The nurse deftly caught it in a basin. The experience was one of the worst in his life so far, worse even than awakening after the amputation.

The nurse wiped him clean and fed him two pills. He slid back into sleep of a sort. When he woke again it seemed only seconds later but the last of the daylight had faded and his headache was slightly less. A different nurse was doing something beside his bed. 'What happened to me?' he asked.

'You can't remember? Don't worry, it'll probably all come back to you if you don't fret about it. The doctor will be in to see you soon.' Her tone was carefully non-committal.

Almost immediately the nurse was replaced by a stern-looking woman in a business suit and carrying a clipboard. 'You're the doctor?' Tim asked her.

She shook her head impatiently and asked him whether he had BUPA. The remainder of her questions seemed to be directed towards whether the hospital would be reimbursed by the NHS for any special consideration that he was granted. Such rapacity, he felt, might well have been left until he felt more able to cope even if he had to be left on a trolley in the corridor until his status was clarified.

The next lady in what seemed to be becoming a queue wore a white coat and introduced herself as Dr Wainwright. Tim ignored the fact that she was into middle age and becoming fat, he was glad to see her anyway. 'How did I come to be in here?' he asked.

She smiled and shook her head. 'There are one or two

people outside who may be able to help you with that in return for answers to some questions. I'm only concerned with your physical condition. You seem to have had a knock on the head.'

'I can't argue with that. I feel as if I've been exchanging headbutts with one of those mountain goats.'

She shook her head. 'The wound would have been nearer the front,' she said. Tim recalled from his earlier hospitalization that most doctors' senses of humour are heavily disguised or stop short where their professions begin.

He found that he had been tucked in with a thoroughness that almost precluded all movement but he managed to drag one arm clear. When he tried to put up a hand to the area that most of his remaining pain was coming from the doctor only said, 'I wouldn't advise it,' and continued listening to his heartbeat. She concluded by shining a torch into his eyes. 'You'll live,' she said. She rose and disappeared in the direction in which Tim had concluded that there had to be a doorway. 'You can see him now,' she said, 'but don't get him excited.'

Raising his head was still beyond his strength and there was a locker blocking some of his vision, but footsteps soon resolved themselves into those of Ann with a uniformed female police sergeant. Was he the only male left alive? Perhaps aliens had carried off every male creature but he, being unconscious, had been missed. They took the visitors' chairs, going out of his sight, all but their talking heads.

'How do you feel?' Ann asked quietly. She seemed tear-stained but he guessed that she was making a special effort to be brave. Even in his bemused condition he was flattered that she should be so anxious.

'Bloody awful,' he said. 'But we already knew that. What I want to know is *why* I feel bloody awful. What happened to me?'

'That's what we all want to know,' said the officer. She had a sweet voice but with a lisp that must, Tim thought, have detracted seriously from her authority.

'This is Brionie Phelps,' Ann said. 'She's a detective sergeant.' Tim had the impression that detectives usually wore plain clothes. He guessed that the DSgt, who was young for her rank and noticeably attractive, preferred to wear uniform to reinforce her authority and to counter the effects of the lisp, her youth, her unmistakeable femininity and a degree of prettiness.

Tim and DSgt Phelps exchanged a smile and a nod. Tim's smile was no more than a token. 'You don't remember anything?' Ms Phelps asked.

'Not a damn thing. I was working in my garden and then suddenly I was here.' He considered trying a little humour along the lines of *the attack of the killer tomatoes*, but decided that it would be out of place.

The detective sergeant opened a briefcase and produced a sheet of closely-typed paper. 'I'll read from the statement that Miss Erskine made,' she said. 'Then you'll know as much as any of us. I'll leave out the preamble that our lawyers insist on. It only says who she is and that she's been staying as your guest. Her statement begins "I was working in the kitchen making preparations for our evening meal. I looked out once and saw Mr Russell holding a long stem of couch-grass and looking down at it. Just a few seconds later I heard a sound that I could not and still cannot identify but my nearest guess would be a whoosh. Mr Russell's dog, Umber, began barking. I looked out again and Mr Russell was lying face down in the mud. I ran outside and rolled him over and made sure he could breathe. Then I went back inside and phoned for an ambulance. While I waited I went out again with a basin and a cloth and wiped blood and mud away from his face and mouth. I had been thinking that he had had a stroke or a faint but now I noticed that he had a serious wound high on the back of his head. It was bleeding steadily and I could see the surface of his skull showing through. I sat down on the ground and took his head on my lap to keep him out of the mud." That's all of it.'

'I was rather relieved,' Ann said. Her voice was both faint and husky. Tim judged that she had shed tears and that they were still not very far away. 'I'm not a doctor but I think it might be easier to recover from a bonk on the head than from a stroke or a cerebral haemorrhage.'

'Well done and ten thousand thanks. I couldn't be happier that you were there.' Tim's wits were returning to him. 'What were you wearing?'

'The other pair of new jeans,' Ann said, 'and it's all right, they need the stiffness washed out of them.'

'I didn't want you to spoil your new yellow dress.'

She laughed at him. 'Silly! I'm wearing it now.'

Tim's muscles still refused to lift his head but by rolling his head and eyes to the side he managed to bring more of her into his field of vision. 'So you are! My eyes don't seem to be focusing very well.'

Ann and Ms Phelps exchanged a startled glance. Ann got up and left the room, walking quickly. 'What's got into her?' Tim asked.

'One minute.' Ms Phelps pretended to be very busy with her notebook until Ann returned, towing the doctor along by her sleeve. The doctor recovered her dignity and her sleeve but not without an effort. 'What's this I hear about a lack of focus?'

'I only said that I wasn't focusing very well,' Tim said plaintively.

'And quite enough too,' said the doctor. 'You two, out; and no visiting until tomorrow morning. Phone first.' She chivvied Tim's two visitors along the corridor.

'Look after Umber for me,' Tim called after them. A voice replied 'Of course,' and he thought that it was Ann's. 'And the house,' he shouted. He gained no reply and the shout hurt his head and brought nausea very close again.

The doctor returned a few minutes later, accompanied by a porter with a trolley. Tim was relieved to see the male porter – at least he no longer felt alone, cast adrift in a female world. The doctor examined his pupils with a pencil torch. 'I'm sending you in for a scan,' she said.

'Your inability to focus may be an outcome of concussion but it could possibly be an indication of something more serious. I'd rather make sure than have that daughter of yours sue me later.'

'I don't have a daughter.'

'Then that young lady . . .?'

'Is no relative,' Tim admitted.

The doctor looked at him with more interest. 'She seemed very upset. Be good to her.'

'I am always good to the better looking girls,' Tim said.

'So am I,' said the porter.

'Men!' said the doctor.

Tim took no interest in the by-play. His mind was clouding again. He was loaded into a waiting ambulance. He was aware of the movement of the ambulance but he had arrived at a passive state. He would submit to whatever anybody decided to do to him but the idea of taking decisions or positive action had become remote from him. He decided, as he subsided into sleep again, that vegetables had the right idea.

EIGHT

The ambulance carried Tim to the infirmary where he was manoeuvred onto a mechanical table and photographed from a variety of angles. He was then left to sleep. Unusually, he was aware of being asleep and enjoyed the sensation. He was woken when the ambulance set off on its return journey an hour later.

The delay had allowed various specialists to study his scans and the reports travelled with him, but the whole trip was still, in his opinion, a waste of resources because the result was indeterminate. No fracture to his skull was visible but there might, he was told seriously, be a hairline crack that did not show up. There did not seem to be any bleeding. It was possible that the interference with his vision might derive from bruising that had caused a small swelling on the brain. It was almost certainly, said the doctor, of only temporary significance but he would be kept in for observation. Tim, who was feeling nauseous again and whose headaches were appearing and vanishing like unwelcome relatives at a funeral, had no objection to waiting in medical care until his symptoms had abated. A nurse inserted a cannula in his wrist and put a handset beside him. Pressure on the handset, she explained, would give him a shot of painkiller.

He had not expected a good night's sleep in a strange and harder bed, especially after the sleeping that he had done during the day and with all the hospital noises around him. Also he was in the habit of sleeping on his side which the bandages on his wound made virtually impossible. However, the bed had as many electrical adjustments as a Formula One car and in fact, once he had it perfectly adjusted with his shoulders and knees raised to suit his own requirements, he slept well but only to wake up with his headaches renewed. He summoned a shot of painkiller.

For the first time he was able to assimilate the room that he was in. It was generously sized for single bed occupancy, cleanly styled, equipped and decorated for its purpose. It had a better than average outlook across a pleasantly informal stretch of garden to a group of houses and a large stand of deciduous trees. In the far distance, beyond a straggle of villages, he could almost make out his own home. The room was well equipped even to a colour television set presented by the local Round Table, but he found later that during his absence the remote control had gone for a walk to some other ward. The one less comforting feature was a track along the middle of the ceiling with an electrical trolley that he could only interpret as a hoist for moving a body complete with coffin. He shied away from the thought that this might be a ward devoted to patients whose prognosis was short.

The presence of a uniformed officer seemed to form a pass for admission without any need to wait for formal visiting hours, so the expected visit by Ann and Brionie occurred while the breakfast dishes were still being cleared. Each was eager to discuss his symptoms in intimate detail but Tim refused. If he did not think about the headaches, the occasional nausea and the perpetual sleepiness they could all be ignored. 'Talk about something else,' he said.

'What I came to talk about is what happened to you,' Brionie said. 'Are you strong enough to talk about that?'

'I'd prefer it. I'm strong enough but totally ignorant. I probably know even less about it than either of you.'

'Perhaps,' Brionie said. Tim judged that she was trying hard to make a show of confidence but feeling a little overwhelmed and hiding it beneath a show of humour. It occurred to him that Ann had just as much cause to feel cast adrift and when he looked with more percipient eyes he thought that the two young women were beginning to cling for mutual support. 'And perhaps not. I'm coming to this case cold and on my own.

'My chiefs have been hit by an outbreak of petty crime plus an indecent assault, a fresh outbreak of burglaries and a possibly unsuccessful bank fraud. They can handle those in-house but that's quite enough. If what happened to you was an accident or a minor assault that was not meant to cause serious harm, well and good. So I'm to make enquiries and report. If it was an attempted murder, I'm to say so; but I may as well explain to you, strictly between ourselves, that if it was an assault it's been strongly hinted that I should utter several short but impassioned prayers that it was little more than a practical joke that went wrong. Otherwise outside help will have to be requested, which is always a very unpopular move, politically and financially. This is my first solo case since I transferred to CID and the wrong moves would not do my career any good at all. So if what happened to you was the outcome of carelessness, a piece of malice that went wrong, something falling out of the sky or anything else short of attempted murder, please say so.'

There was an empty pause. Tim had nothing to say so he said it.

'Oh dear! I've visited your house,' Brionie continued, 'and Ann showed me exactly where you were lying. Your doctor could not give an opinion as to what hit you but spoke vaguely about a hammer. Ann is quite sure that there was nobody near enough to you to club you. Much of the patch of earth around you had been freshly turned over but apart from your own footprints there were those of Ann and of the ambulance men. Those were easily identified where they survived and there seems to have been nobody else near you. Would you agree?'

Tim had been prepared to coast along and to let other people do the worrying, but now he found himself forced to think and wonder. 'Up to the point at which my memory cuts off, yes. I don't recall seeing anybody except Ann, who was at the kitchen window, before suddenly waking up in here with the headache to end them all. But whether there's a blank patch during which somebody approached me with a golf club or something and whacked me over the head I have no idea. I rather think not.'

Brionie was nodding. 'In case there is something missing, the doctor says that your memory may come back if you relax and wait for it. And what is your last recollection of seeing Ann?'

'She went in to prepare a meal. If you include seeing her through the kitchen window, I think I saw her only a very few seconds before I blacked out. She seemed to be rolling pastry. That was the last memory I can recall. I remember thinking what a pretty and domestic picture it made.'

Ann looked at him, slightly flustered, but she smiled their private smile. 'I ought to explain that I went in to prepare the evening meal but I had time in hand so I was making a tart to put by for tomorrow. If they keep you in here I my have to eat it all myself or give some of it to Umber, because pastry doesn't freeze well. I looked up from rolling pastry to see him lying in the mud,' she said. 'So that surely closes the gap. I mean, we saw each other while I was rolling pastry, so that doesn't allow time for much of a gap.'

Brionie studied Ann for a few seconds before switching her gaze to Tim. 'You mentioned a golf club. What put that into your mind?'

'I have no idea. I don't play golf. I just had difficulty imagining anything else.'

Brionie studied him for a few moments before going on, 'You were not near enough to the boundary wall for anyone to have crept up on you behind it. But Ann says that your dog was looking towards the boundary wall and that you were working away from the wall and so your back was towards it. The blow seems to have arrived from behind you. What's more, your dog didn't bark, so I think we can disregard hand-held weapons. But that leaves us with some sort of projectile. There were a few stones lying nearby big enough to do that sort of damage.' Brionie paused and Tim saw her face change. 'This is going to take some thinking about. We may have to approach it from the opposite direction. Tell me about your enemies.'

Tim thought of himself as a mild and inoffensive person, a pussycat, everybody's friend. 'I don't think that I have any enemies.'

'That would make you unique.'

'I am,' said Tim.

Ann made a wordless sound of disagreement. 'You are, but you're not as unique as all that. And yes, don't jump down my throat. I know that you can't have degrees of uniqueness. I think you do have enemies,' said Ann. 'There's Mr Waller, for a start, and my stepdad Mr Hooper.'

'Would that be Woodworm Waller?' Brionie asked. 'We would love to put him away. If anything gets stolen around here it usually passes through his hands, but not here and you didn't hear me say that.'

A few minutes were taken up with explaining about Messrs Waller and Hooper. Tim tried to play down the violence whereas Ann relished giving a blow by blow account of each fracas. She seemed proud of Tim's prowess with his fists.

Brionie did not seem shocked. 'Next time you feel like beating up innocent criminals,' she said, 'tip me off first and then I may be able to catch them in a weakened state, but don't just tell me about it afterwards or the Book may require me to do something about it.

'It seems to me that those two gentlemen will have to account for themselves. There may be others. I'd better go and get on with it.' She looked at Ann. 'Do you want a lift back home?'

'Would you mind?' Ann asked Tim. 'It would save me ages, hanging around and waiting for buses that only come when they feel like it. And Umber will be waiting for her dinner and a walk.'

'Go ahead,' Tim said. 'I still have some sleeping to do.'

Ann looked at him with what seemed to be real concern. 'You are going to be all right?'

'As far as I know.' Tim struggled against it but a yawn escaped him. 'In the meantime just carry on. Look after the house and Umber. Let me know if you need money.'

Before his visitors' footsteps had quite died away, Tim slid away into sleep and woke up, hours later, with a foul taste in his mouth and both his headaches raging. He grabbed the handset of the patient-controlled analgesia (PCA) but it would only allow him a single shot. In a few minutes the pains lessened but his mood failed to improve. The question of how he had been injured had seemed academic and unreal but now it was dawning on him for the first time that somebody really had meant to do him mischief, probably even to kill him. He was quite sure that he had done nothing to deserve anything so drastic and it followed therefore that his assailant had been operating out of either spite or self-interest. He felt anger fermenting inside him.

His brooding was interrupted by the arrival of a thin man wearing a grey suit and a dog-collar. He had a full head of carefully coiffed hair and a handsome face spoiled by protruding teeth. 'Let me introduce myself,' he said. He had a fluting voice that Tim found irritating. 'I'm the hospital pastor. What denomination are you?'

'I'm an agnostic with atheistic tendencies,' Tim said.

'Come now,' said the pastor. He advanced all the way to the bedside. 'Were you ever baptised?'

'Probably, but so long ago that it's lost in the mists of time. It didn't take. Please leave me in peace.'

The pastor seemed deaf to Tim's words. He wriggled to make himself as comfortable as he could in the bedside chair. Evidently he was preparing for a long stay. 'If you were baptised then you must be Christian. Catholic or Protestant?'

Tim tried not to explode but he refused to take the easy way out by pretending. 'I never discuss religion,' he said.

'Faith is so precious and so fragile that I would hate to risk damaging anybody else's.'

The pastor's face had the closed look of one who refuses to hear whatever he dislikes. His voice was patronizing. 'I don't think there's much danger of that. Do you believe in God?' he asked abruptly.

Tim found it difficult to specify exactly what he did believe in and he saw no reason why he should be the one to struggle with shades of wording. 'Please define God.'

Without hesitation the pastor replied, 'The supreme being, eternal, all powerful, all knowing, father of Christ the Redeemer.'

'If you had used some such terms as "the sum of all the forces of nature" I might have gone along with you,' Tim said. 'But you're trying to make the case for a personal God, an individual being sitting on high, seeing everything, interfering even in tiny matters but ignoring colossal wars and pestilences. You may say that his actions and motives are far beyond our understanding, but that's more than I can swallow. It defies all imagination and therefore belief. Please go away.'

The pastor glanced out of the window to where rain was now falling out of a black sky. He looked away quickly. 'Surely those very forces of nature are all that you need to convince you of the existence of God. When you go outside and look around you at the trees and flowers, the blue sky and . . . and animals, can you not detect the genius of a great designer?'

Tim knew that by making any reply he was opening the door to argument, but his resistance was wearing down even as his tone was becoming ever more peevish. 'I enjoy what I see but I am perfectly satisfied with a Darwinian explanation of almost everything; and I have no doubt that if science progresses at its present pace the remotest gaps in human knowledge will soon be closed.'

'Even if you don't admit to being a member of a denomination, surely you count yourself a Christian.'

Tim knew that he had already been pushed into breaking

his own resolution. He guessed that general guidance from the church to hospital clergy was never to push the protagonist further than he would willingly go, but the other's persistence allied with his own physical discomfort had already made a controlled explosion inevitable. 'I believe,' he said firmly, 'that Christ was a real person, but documents emerging, especially among the Dead Sea Scrolls, suggest that he was more a political agitator, preaching against the Roman occupiers, than a religious leader. Anyway, at that time the Romans never crucified anyone only for their religious beliefs. Later, Saul of Tarsus suffered a stroke on the way to Damascus and had hallucinations that he took very seriously. He later wrote and preached his own version of the New Testament story and his version became generally accepted. It seems to have sprung out of nowhere, decades after the death of Christ.'

As Tim spoke, the pastor's face lost its look of self-satisfaction and became scandalized. His voice went up and a bony finger was thrust almost into Tim's face. 'Who has been feeding you this modern claptrap? The Bible is the Bible and the Scriptures are the Scriptures and that's an end to the matter. What you're saying is blasphemy!'

Once started, Tim was not going to retreat. 'What's blasphemous about it? Truth can never be blasphemous. Surely you know that at or about the time of Christ there were several rather better supported rival sects with their own leaders, almost every one of them claiming to be a son of God. If God is so all-powerful it can't be beyond his capability to father more than one son.'

The pastor leaped to his feet. 'Name some of these rivals if you can.' His voice was being raised to a screech and his face was aflame.

As it happened, Tim had studied the subject for a passage in a previous novel and his interest had been caught enough for him to pursue the subject further by way of the Internet. For once his memory for names allowed instant recall and the pleasure of needling this intransigent person seemed to be relieving his headaches. 'John the Baptist,' he said. 'Simon Magus. Apollonius. Simon Bar Kochba, Gnosticism. In fact, if it hadn't been for the conversion of the Emperor Constantine we might now be worshipping Mithras or Isis.'

The pastor uttered a squawk. 'You're twisting history to suit your own ends. I think you must be the Antichrist!'

It was just as the pastor raised his voice in his denunciation of Tim and Tim's every word and thought that there was the sound of feet in the passage and Ann made her return. 'Mr Downing!' she exclaimed. 'What are you doing here?'

Again Tim's recall worked with unprecedented speed. 'This was the only job he could get after running off with your mother,' he said. The name had been lurking somewhere in his subconscious.

Mr Downing also was enlightened. 'So you're the sinner who debauched this young girl!'

That stung Tim. 'That's the pot calling the kettle black with a vengeance,' he said. He spoke gently so that his words had all the more sting. 'If any debauchery was practised it was by you. I only gave her a roof over her head after you seduced her mother and she was left homeless and almost penniless. I have nothing but contempt for the way that you, a supposed Christian, treated her. I have never laid a finger on her and if you dare to suggest otherwise I'll take you to court – or flatten your face for you.'

Downing's face went from red to white and he began to gobble like a turkey. Before he could formulate a reply, Ann had jumped in front of him. She barely came up to his chin but she glared – up his nose, Tim thought later. 'He could do it, too,' she said. 'And it's quite true that he hasn't touched me. And even if he had, I'm past the age of consent. I think you're horrible. Horrible.'

Tim, who was already suffering pangs of conscience, half expected the other to swell up and curse him by bell, book and candle, summoning all the less forgiving angels to sweep him away or conjuring up demons to his own support, but either Downing lacked such backup or else he had become demoralized. He was out of the room and his footsteps were stamping away along the corridor before Ann could draw breath again. He seemed to be talking to himself or possibly to some celestial being, possibly to God.

'How dare he?' Ann demanded of the ceiling. Tim was surprised to see tears again on her cheeks. 'How dare he come here, all holier-than-thou, and carry on as though you were the sinner, when he ran off with my mother, just as you said, and never gave me a thought, and you've been the good Samaritan all the way, taking me in and helping me and refusing any kind of return or reward.' She paused and dried her eyes on the corner of a sheet. She even produced the ghost of a smile. 'All the same, if seducing means what I think it means, I expect my mum did most of it. She always seemed to have more go in her than he did even if she couldn't direct it. Don't look so sad,' she added, 'I don't think he'll come back again after the earful we both gave him.'

Tim sighed deeply. 'I'm sad because he provoked me into doing what I was determined not to do and saying what I didn't want to say. I have my own philosophy and much of it is quite compatible with the teachings of the church. Where the two don't mesh together, who am I to say that I'm right and they're wrong?'

'I'm sure you are and they are,' she said. 'You sound more like somebody who knows what he's talking about. But never mind.'

'I do mind. And who enlightened you about the age of consent?'

'That's another never-mind.' She seated herself in the chair vacated by Mr Downing, 'And now the good news. Do you want to hear it?'

'Of course.'

'Umber still misses you. She spends half the day going from room to room, to see if you've come back yet. All

the same, I haven't let her training slip back. I took her
on a walk as far as the Victory Park early this morning
and I decided to push her training a bit further, so I sat
her and walked on a bit. And I bumped into the lady who
runs the kennels. We walked and talked for ages. She'd
been visited recently by the burglar and she was not
pleased, let me tell you. It seemed kindest to let her blow
off steam. And then I suddenly realized that I'd left poor
Umber sitting alone for ages and ages until she was just
a speck in the distance and she'd never moved, so I whis-
tled and she came tearing along and skidded to a halt in
front of me, sitting and waiting patiently for her little
biscuit and looking very relieved. The lady was most
impressed.'

'So am I. That's very good. Keep it up. Steadiness is
vital in a gun dog. The police seem to tolerate unsteadi-
ness in police dog training, but it can never be tolerated
in the shooting field because a dog that charges ahead will
either get shot or disturb all the wildlife in the next bit.'

'I'll tell you something that's not so good. Can you
take it?' she asked anxiously.

'It can't be so very bad. You looked quite happy when
you first arrived.'

'It's not so terribly awful. It seems sort of funny in a
macabre sort of way. When I left with Brionie Phelps to
get a lift home, she sat in the car without driving off and
asked a lot of questions. She worded them very carefully,
trying to find out what she could without giving away
what she was thinking. But I'm not as green as I'm
cabbage-looking—'

'Not by a mile,' Tim said. 'And you're not so very
cabbage-looking. Only a little bit.'

'Thank you. Anyway, I sussed what she was thinking.
She thinks that I'm probably the only person who could
walk up behind you without alarming you. She thinks I
may have done that and bonked you on the head with
one of the garden tools or something. The rolling pin
wouldn't be at all the right shape for your wound but

they've taken it away for examination by the forensic people all the same. As if I'd do such a thing to you of all people.'

Tim was tempted to laugh but he thought that it might make his head hurt worse. 'Don't worry about it. I was very hungry so I was glancing towards you every few seconds to see when you were going to signal me that the meal was ready. You wouldn't have had time. Anyway, why would you do a thing like that? I can't see that you'd have anything to gain.'

'That's what she was trying to find out.'

'Unless I've done or said something to infuriate you?'

Her faced changed. He thought that she might be going to cry. 'Don't be silly! You never could. Quite the reverse. Don't even think such a thing.' She leaned forward suddenly and laid her cheek – a wet cheek, he noticed – against his.

Before allowing her to leave to catch her bus, Tim put her through an inquisition, but it was soon clear that she was coping well with all the ramifications of house-keeping and looking after Umber at least to the standard of most dog owners. She had even brought him in a small parcel of clean pyjamas and handkerchiefs. She had included the book that he had been reading in bed and his Ipod with all his favourite music on it. She had even remembered the battery charger.

As he settled down to sleep Tim recited to himself, '"As if I'd do such a thing to you of all people!"' And he fell asleep smiling through his headache, with the Ipod playing Scarlatti into his unreceptive ears.

NINE

Tim might have been in danger of losing track of the passing days. He slept and woke, sometimes feeling better and sometimes worse. Sometimes his mind was clouded; sometimes it was sharp. He was given medication and his dressings were replaced. He began to relearn the knack, forgotten since the days of his amputation, of peeing into a bottle without wetting the bed. The pains became less and the patient controlled analgesia was removed. Sometimes when he awoke it was dark and that was the only demarcation of night time. There was a clock on the wall opposite his bed and if he bothered to read it he could usually guess whether it was morning except when the time was between seven and ten. Mealtimes usually gave him a clue. Cereal and toast meant breakfast, soup only turned up as a precursor to lunch and the evening meal was more akin to high tea. He never had much appetite but he welcomed the meals as a measure of passing time.

After a few days – he had lost count of how many – his mind cleared. He suddenly snapped back into awareness of all that was happening to and around him.

Ann was a faithful visitor. Sometimes she came alone and sometimes she was accompanied by DSgt Brionie Phelps, the latter usually in uniform but sometimes looking very young and girlish in a summer frock or jeans and a jumper.

After the hasty departure of the Reverend Mr Downing, Ann made several solo visits before Tim again saw DSgt Phelps. She brought Ann with her but Tim had Ann to himself while Brionie was parking the car.

When they had exchanged greetings Ann said, 'I've never seen your leg without its foot.'

'I've tried to keep it hidden. I was afraid that it might shock you.'

'I'm bound to see it some time and I don't want it to come as a shock. I wouldn't want to hurt your feelings if I said the wrong thing.'

That seemed reasonable to Tim. The hospital staff had been regarding his stump so matter-of-factly that he had come to think of it as unremarkable. He drew his leg out from under the bedclothes and pulled up his pyjama trouser-leg and he was surprised when Ann gasped. 'The rest of you is so perfect,' she said. 'Perhaps it will prevent the gods from loving you so much that they'll steal you away. Like putting a mistake into the pattern of a carpet,' she added obscurely.

'It doesn't shock you?'

'Not the least bit.' She ducked her head suddenly and kissed the smooth skin of his stump. He did not feel the caress – scar tissue has no nerves – but he saw a tear left behind. It was a moment of high emotion but Brionie chose it to arrive from the car park, very smart in her uniform. Tim put his leg away. He could see little sign of constraint between the two visitors.

'I can see you both privately if you like,' Brionie said, 'but it might be more convenient if I saw you together. Is that all right?'

'That would be best,' Tim said. 'We aren't concocting any stories between us and we may refresh each other's memories.'

Ann nodded. Brionie produced a small tape recorder, started it running and placed it on the locker together with a notebook and pencil. Tim wondered what would be the female equivalent of 'belt and braces'. There was plenty of room for speculation.

'Have you remembered any more?' Brionie asked.

Tim was enjoying one of his more lucid periods. 'I still don't think that there is any more to remember,' he said. 'One moment I was pulling up weeds. I remember that I kept glancing at the kitchen window, waiting for the signal to come in to dinner. I could see Ann at her pastry making. I knew that we were due to eat and pastry takes time, so I concluded that she was making a pie or tart for later. Then suddenly I was in here with my head hurting like hell. In between there was only an instant. It was like the instantaneous flick from one shot to another in a film. No time at all.'

'So far as you remember.'

'So far as I remember.'

'And in that instant?'

'Nothing. Am I not making it clear? The time just was not there. I think perhaps there was a sound, but that would have been in the microsecond before I blacked out.' He looked at Ann. She was very easy on the eye. She had brushed her hair out but the natural curls had taken over again. She had bought a new dress in autumnal colours suited to the coming season and to her own colouring and she could well have featured on the cover of a magazine or the lid of a chocolate box. He thought that she must be gaining confidence in her choice of clothes. 'Did you . . .?' he asked her. 'But you were behind glass, you wouldn't have heard much.'

'Umber heard something. I saw her look up.'

'You're right,' Tim said. 'So she did. But that was at the very moment when I was struck, at least I think so. And that suggests that there's no time missing from my memory.' He screwed his face up with the effort of recall.

'The doctor said that you mustn't struggle to remember,' Ann pointed out. 'You must let things come back of their own accord.'

'That's what I'm doing,' said Tim, 'and all that comes back to me is a hiss. Or possibly a whistle. The sort of sound that I imagine an arriving projectile might make. I think you described it to me as a whoosh!'

'As you said, I was behind glass – double glazing in fact. The sound was very muffled. And now you're making me sound as though I don't want you to remember.'

There was a moment of uncomfortable silence.

'What you're saying suggests a subsonic projectile,' said Brionie. 'You don't hear a supersonic projectile coming. And anyway, a supersonic projectile would probably have knocked your brains out. Ann suggested an arrow. A friend of mine who belongs to an archery club said that an arrow can make the same sort of noise but it wouldn't make that shape of wound. I took a photograph to the professor of pathology and he agreed that the wound was typical of a medium-weight projectile travelling fast but very slowly compared to the speed of a bullet and striking a glancing blow, but he couldn't or wouldn't put any figures to it and he added that a joiner's claw-hammer would have done similar damage. He said that the blow came from behind but whether it was struck horizontally or steeply downward or anything in between he couldn't say. It would depend whether you were stooping or standing up straight. Which would it be?'

'After this time? I haven't the faintest idea. When you're weeding, you go up and down all the time.'

'I must say this, even if it makes me look guilty or like an idiot. I'm quite sure that nobody came near him,' Ann said. 'And Umber would have flown at anybody who raised a hammer near Mr Russell. But she just looked puzzled. Like this.' Ann's face assumed the expression of a puzzled Labrador. It was very convincing.

'Tell me quite honestly,' Brionie said to Ann, 'hypothetically how would the dog have reacted if you had raised a hammer near Mr Russell?'

'Hypothetically, I don't bloody know,' Ann said. It was the first time that Tim had heard her use anything but the blandest language. The suggestion was rubbing her on the raw.

Tim was still aware of the soreness of his head but now, when he homed his senses in on it, he could not find any clue to the weapon that had caused it. It certainly did not feel as though it had been made by a joiner's hammer, or by anything else in particular and definitely not by a rolling pin. 'Had you thought of a large calibre bullet which had already been deformed and lost some of its energy by passing through a deer? A stalker on the high ground miles away might aim for a skull shot but put his bullet through the soft part of the neck instead. It would have been travelling much more slowly by the time it reached here.'

'There are two objections to that as a theory,' said Brionie Phelps. 'One: a deformed bullet spins in the air and makes an unforgettable, whirring noise or the whine of a ricochet. Secondly: a thorough search of your garden and the neighbourhood produced nothing of the least interest. Thousands of stones, of course, that might have been projected from some sort of catapult – far too many to examine them all individually for traces of skin and hair.'

'A deformed bullet makes a lot of noise,' said Tim. As a student he had spent some time and earned some money butt-marking for the Territorials. 'I don't think that a ball would be noisy. A projectile could have bounced over into the field.'

'Ann says that your dog was looking towards the field; and from the way that you fell it looks as though you were struck a glancing blow from that direction. The projectile would have hit the wall of your house or gone past it into the road.'

'I hope you're saving all those stones for me,' Tim said.

Brionie looked at him as though he had begun to gibber. 'What on earth would you want them for?'

'They're part of the soil structure of my garden. They hold the moisture through the dry weather, when we get any. I don't know how, but that's unimportant. The fact that it happens is what matters. If you take all the stones out of soil it dries out quickly and plants die.'

Brionie made a note. 'I never knew that, about stones holding the moisture. I have dozens of potato sacks of them. I'll leave them for you. My helpful professor of pathology gave me lunch in the staff club and he induced a senior lecturer in physics and a lecturer in anatomy to join us.'

She looked up and smiled. 'The professor is trying very hard to claim the cost of the lunches, by the way, but so far no luck. They spent an hour drawing diagrams on envelopes and doing complex calculations and they concluded that to produce the level of damage that you suffered by means of a catapult-type weapon would take something too large to be carried secretly and the thickness of rubber required to accelerate a stone over the span of a man's arms and give it enough energy to do that damage would be more than the average human could pull.

'So we're no further forward. I coaxed one of our forensic scientists to lend me a Luminal spray and I sprayed it around in the area that seemed most likely from what Ann told me. We got some areas of luminescence indicating blood, but that was mostly where your head had been after you had been hit.'

'Not much help from forensic science, then,' Tim said.

'None,' said Brionie. 'But I've been allowed to keep my pair of beat bobbies and they're going from door to door to find out who saw or heard what, and when, and whether anybody had picked up anything other than a common stone that could have formed a projectile. A fragment of spent asteroid, perhaps – they hunt for them in the Australian desert, I'm told, where the surface hasn't been disturbed for hundreds of years. We'll see what, if anything, those enquiries turn up.' She sighed and made some more notes. 'There's one thing I must check with the astronomy department at the university. A comet is mostly ice. I've heard of comet debris reaching the earth although most of it probably melts and boils away on entering the atmosphere. But there must be a between stage when it's just cold and solid enough to make it as far as earth. It might be possible for a lump of that to have smitten you and then have melted away.'

'I have to give you credit for your imagination,' Ann said. 'And for your restraint. You've never once uttered a word of complaint at my stupidity in washing out the wound while I waited for the ambulance.'

Brionie smiled and shrugged. 'You weren't to know. Medically, you may have been quite right. But an analysis of the contents of the wound might have been helpful.'

Tim had found that, since his injury, his mind became clouded by tiredness more quickly than ever before. The search for credible explanations for what had befallen him he found particularly tiring. Before slipping back into a refreshing doze, however, he thought to ask, 'You've got no satisfaction from interviewing our possible suspects, then?'

Brionie Phelps made a face. 'Quite the reverse in fact. I would be breaking every rule if I repeated what any suspect had told me but I'll go so far as to say that satisfaction is not what I got.'

'Then you have eliminated Ann from your list of suspects?'

Brionie looked uncomfortable. 'I must have been less subtle than I thought I was. I never did suspect her but I have to go through the process for eliminating her, not as a suspect but as a red herring for a defence counsel to use, if we ever get that far. If defence counsel tries to deflect suspicion in her direction, I want to be able to say that she was thoroughly investigated and proved innocent. Anyway, how could I suspect her when she's obviously . . .?'

'Obviously what?'

'Oh, I forget what I was going to say. Have you thought of anything else?'

'I made another enemy recently,' Tim said. 'The hospital God-botherer called on me. He wouldn't accept that I never argue religion, my reason being that I wouldn't want to damage anything as precious and fragile as somebody's faith, but in the end – and I like to feel that it was because I was making such a good case for evolutionary theory – he lost his temper and called me the Antichrist. And he turned out to be Ann's wicked stepfather. Well, not quite that because as far as I know her mother's second marriage is still valid; but I'm referring to the local minister who ran off with Ann's mother. He disappeared immediately from his parish, presumably dismissed but not unfrocked, and I suppose that the hospital position was all that was open to him. I don't think he believed me when I assured him that I had never laid a finger on her.'

'He was looking as black as a thundercloud when I arrived on the scene,' Ann said. 'And he looked at me as though I was the ultimate scarlet woman.'

Tim smiled grimly. 'I don't remember whether I said aloud that he was the pot calling the kettle black or that he was judging other people by his own standards, but I dare say that my expression said it all.'

'As mine would certainly have done. Don't quote me on this,' Brionie said, 'but I wish I'd been a fly on the wall. I've always wondered why a belief in a rather unlikely scenario involving the supernatural should qualify somebody to assume moral superiority, lay down the law for me over and over and to bore me out of my skull in the process by endless repetition.'

Tim pulled his wits together. '"*What I tell you three times is true*." But that's absolutely by the way. We can't count the allegedly Reverend Mr Downing as a suspect because he didn't even know of my existence until after I was struck down.'

A frown was sitting uncomfortably on Ann's usually tranquil face. 'That may not be quite true,' she said. 'Mr Downing was always pally with my stepfather. They used to meet up and tut about the wickedness of the younger generation over a glass of beer or sweet sherry. I can't see them missing a golden opportunity to . . . to misunderstand when you were so . . .' Her voice died away and she sniffed.

'There's something quite biblical,' Tim said hastily, 'about being struck down by a mysterious bolt from heaven. Do you think there's something in the power of prayer after all?'

Ann managed a shaky laugh. 'I think Brionie's watching you to see if it happens again.'

'If it does,' Brionie said, 'we'll have the answers to two questions – about the power of prayer and how you came to be struck down. And we'll all have to walk more carefully in future.'

'We needn't worry about Ann and I,' said Tim. 'I can't speak for you, but we haven't sinned. Not, at least, in that respect. Not even in coveting my neighbour's ass, so far as I can remember – in either the British or the American sense of the word.'

Brionie tried but failed to suppress a snort of amusement. She was trying to frame an innocent but amusing answer when they were interrupted by the arrival of another woman. 'Ah, there you are!' she said. 'I've been looking all over the place for you. I didn't know the patient's name, so in the end, I had to go back to the main door and get a very nice young man to phone around the wards to find a sister who knew where you were.'

'Hallo, Mum!' Ann exclaimed glumly.

TEN

Ann's mother was a dainty woman despite turning fleshy in her forties. She was dressed in what was definitely a summer frock, silky and thin, although the weather, in deference to the passing seasons, was noticeably cooler – she brought a breath of cold air in with her and she had visible goose-pimples. Her face was reverting to the chubbiness of a baby-face but with a pout to the lips and a twinkle in the eye that no baby could achieve. Her hair looked naturally blonde though it did not have the natural curl of her daughter's, and her legs, in thin nylon, led the eye from high heels to high hemline. She was a walking invitation to appreciative whistles. Beyond the whistles, attraction would have to be in the eye of the beholder, because seen beside her daughter she was noticeably lacking in the bounce and juiciness of youth. Tim soon decided that word of great skill in the arts of the bedchamber must have passed from man to man to explain her popularity. She treated Ann to a quick kiss on the cheek and then took over the only visitor's chair with any pretension to comfort. Brionie fetched another chair from the corridor.

'My love!' Mrs Hooper exclaimed, 'I've been looking for you all over the place. And I couldn't find my way back to the main door to find out where you were, I had to ask a doctor the way. Where were you hiding, for these past months? And is this the young man I've been hearing about?'

Ann got in first with the question that both Brionie and Tim were eager to ask. 'Hearing about from who?' she demanded.

'Hearing what?' Tim added.

'The news is all over the place. I'm happy for you but aren't you a little young?'

Ann was not about to let her mother get away with vague insinuations. 'Young for what?'

'You know very well what I mean.'

'I'm afraid I do. But it hasn't been happening and anyway the law says that I'm old enough.'

'Does it, dear?' From her tone, Mrs Hooper seemed to find the statement significant.

Tim was unhappy about the direction the conversation was taking. 'The law also says that you can kiss my feet but that doesn't mean that you've ever done it.'

Mrs Hooper seemed unable to assimilate a point made in this oblique manner. She gave a girlish giggle quite unsuited to her age or appearance. She was sitting carelessly or perhaps deliberately showing a lot of leg. 'What a funny idea! Have you asked her to do that?'

'No,' Tim said firmly. 'I have not.'

'And you are?'

'I'm Tim Russell.'

'And you are the young man my daughter's living with?'

That remark was so filled with erroneous implications that Tim had difficulty formulating an answer. Ann saved him by speaking first. 'Mother, Mr Russell kindly offered me a home when you went off and left me with nowhere to go. And he has been kindness itself and a perfect gentleman. He hasn't asked me to kiss his feet but if he did ask me I'd do it.'

Mrs Hooper's forehead suffered an unaccustomed crease. 'I thought Mr Hooper was going to look after you.'

'And you can guess what sort of looking after he may have had in mind. He's a religious crank. He suggested, just once, that I should come with you when you moved in with him. I think his intention was to sacrifice my virginity on the nearest convenient altar.' (Tim for a moment was struck with admiration for the turn of phrase.

Ann would make a useful companion for a novelist.) 'And your back was hardly turned before Mr Hooper was selling the house.'

'Well that was just too bad of them both. I wasn't going to put up with the sort of treatment I was getting so I'm on my own again now. I've found a nice little flat off the High Street and I want you to come back and stay with me while we get all this sorted out.'

Ann looked anxiously at Tim, who said, 'There's nothing to sort out. We're perfectly happy the way we are and perfectly legal too.' Ann sent him a glowing look.

From far away along the corridor came the sound of footsteps and even raised voices, most unsuited to the air of calm and confidence for which hospitals struggle. Ann's mother raised her own voice to match and spoke hastily but seemingly from the heart. 'Come back with me now, dear, and we'll see about settling you in. This arrangement really isn't proper.'

Ann looked from Tim to Brionie to her mother, who was in a noticeably nervous state. 'When were you so concerned with propriety?' she asked.

Mrs Hooper spoke quickly, almost gabbling. 'I would like to see you properly married. After that, your business is yours and your husband's.'

Tim had for some years avoided all mention of marriage; indeed, even a hint about the subject had been the downfall of one of his lady friends. But now, at one of the least propitious moments, it seemed to be the most attractive goal. It was also a subject that might shut up these annoying persons who were buzzing like flies around his throbbing head. 'If you are referring to Ann and myself,' he said firmly, 'the question of marriage has not yet been discussed. It would have been too early. But I'm in no doubt that the subject will come up very soon. When it does,' he said to Ann, 'how will you feel . . .?'

Ann had been blushing a delicate pink. Her innermost thoughts were being dragged into the daylight. She took two steps forward and squatted beside the bed, laying her cheek against his. He felt her cheek crease in a smile. 'This is not the romantic occasion . . .' she began in a whisper.

'No,' he said, also whispering. 'It isn't. But it's important that we both know . . . For my part, I can't imagine anything happier than . . .'

'Nor can I.' At last each of them had managed to finish a whole sentence. As she pulled away and stood up she managed, as if by accident, to brush her lips across his cheek. This was the first physical contact of any intimacy between them and, at the soft warmth of it, Tim felt a jolt of something like electricity leap from his cheek to his loins, taking in several other organs on the way.

The sounds in the corridor had resolved themselves into the patter of a nurse's feet, the heavier thumps of the ward sister, the measured pacing of a neatly and formally dressed man carrying a briefcase and the angry clumping of Ann's stepfather, Mr Hooper the shop manager, all of which sounds were topped by irritable voices. Ann's mother seemed to lose momentum. Evidently whatever had been behind her anxiety and impatience was now beyond reach. The crowd drew up in a semicircle around the bed. It did not radiate happiness. The presence of Brionie, in uniform for once, hardly seemed to register.

The ward sister, who had protested every inch of the way, fired the opening rounds. 'Mr Russell,' she snapped, 'this is a far larger party of visitors than the rules would allow, even if this had been within visiting hours. If we let every patient get away with flouting the rules, the hospital would be crowded out and we'd never get anything done.'

'Fine by me,' Tim said. 'Throw them out.' The touch of Ann's lips seemed to have banished his headache for the moment but now it was making a return with interest. His retort seemed to have disarmed the sister who left the room, perhaps in search of Security. The nurse went in pursuit.

'Now perhaps I may introduce myself,' said the man with the briefcase. Tim had already recognized the high color, the black hair and the blue jaw. 'I am—'

'Walter Headstone,' said Tim. 'Solicitor and Writer to the Signet. We have played snooker once or twice and we were opponents at bridge once.'

'Quite right,' said Mr Headstone. 'But let me explain that I cling to the rather macabre surname because at least people remember it. Please accept my apology for not recognizing you straight away but at the moment you are somewhat different in appearance from when I last saw you. May I add that I was solicitor and am executor to the estate of the late Angus Tirrell.'

There was a gasp from Ann. 'Late? Uncle Gus is dead? And nobody told me? How could you? At least I could have gone to the funeral. He was a big, big part of my childhood, one of my favorite people in the whole world. He used to take me swimming when Dad was too busy. I suppose the funeral's over and finished with now?'

'I'm afraid so,' said the solicitor. 'He passed away suddenly of a heart attack at about the time when you took to the – ah – wild. But you mustn't put all the blame on your family. There were some attempts to find you but—'

Ann was not to be pacified. 'They couldn't have been very energetic attempts. "Woodworm" Waller ripped me off and you –' she glared at Mr Hooper with so much venom that he stepped back a pace and tried to hide his bulk behind his smaller wife – 'you followed me to Mr Russell's house and even then you didn't say a word.' There was a babble of protest, directed mostly at Mr Hooper but also at Ann's denunciation of the family in general.

All this talking was echoing around in Tim's head to his great discomfort. The patient surely had some rights to peace and quiet, 'Shut up, everybody,' he said. To his amazement they did so. 'Now, tell us why you're here,' he said to the solicitor.

'It's very simple.' Mr Headstone addressed himself to Ann. 'The late Angus Tirrell was your mother's brother but he had no great opinion of his sister's intelligence. Frankly, his opinion as expressed to me was that by the time that you, his only niece, came to inherit, some man would certainly have stripped your mother of her inheritance.' (Ann's mother gave an indignant snort but managed to look faintly gratified. She glanced sidelong at Mr Hooper only to meet his glance in return. Apparently in her mind there was a certain cachet in being any man's prey.) 'So he left her a not ungenerous lump sum and the remainder comes to you.'

'Oh! I always believed that he was rather well off,' Ann said hesitantly.

'You could put it like that. Or you could say that he was just plain rich. It depends on your criteria. He had an excellent business brain. He owned some other properties but in particular he was the sole proprietor of Dingle's, the multiple store.'

Tim had a clear recollection of Dingle's, an overpowering block of stonework in the very heart of the town, adequately provided with nearby parking and filled with retail at its best. Shoppers in search of quality or of the unusual combined with a reliable after-sales service would drive there from neighboring towns. In Dingle's might be found wines from the cheapest to the best but always value for money, the best haircut for a hundred miles around, clothes in current fashion, food to tempt the most fastidious palate. It also ran wedding and similar lists with great efficiency, delivering precisely on the promised day. General opinion was that Dingle's might be marginally more expensive but that it provided remarkable value.

The stunned silence seemed to be stretching on and on. To Tim, it seemed high time that somebody said something. There was only one subject on his mind. 'Miss Erskine and I have just become engaged,' he said into the silence. He paused for a second or two but Ann made no protest. Evidently she accepted their whispers as being a proper exchange of proposal and acceptance. There was a babble of disquiet from the onlookers but it was not verbalized. Nobody wanted to be the first to object to what was obviously a suitable match. For lack of any positive response Tim had to go on. 'I was about to ask that somebody goes to the shops with her to help her choose a ring and see that she got a fair deal, but now it seems that she must own quite a lot of rings.'

'I fear not,' said the solicitor, smiling. 'Most of the more mundane departments – food, household, clothing and so on – are owned by the store but specialist or high-tech departments including jewellery are concessions. The jewellery department in Dingle's is leased and managed by Simon Westrick.'

'Well, that's all right,' Tim said. 'He owes me a favor. He skidded into a ditch last winter and I gave him a lift home.'

Hooper, the shopkeeper, broke his long silence. 'I don't think that you need me any more,' he said. 'I only came along as company for my wife.' Ann's mother looked surprised but said nothing.

'Hold your horses,' said Brionie. She had been a silent observer but now there was a snap to her voice that stopped all chatter and anchored Hooper in his place. 'This changes everything. Your family, Ann, must have known for some time that you have a substantial legacy coming. We don't know what plots may have been hatched to get hands on that legacy, but a relationship between you and a marriageable man would obviously not have been welcomed. And then that marriageable young man suffers an injury that may well have been an attempt at murder. I shall have to report to my superiors. Almost certainly somebody will be put in over my head – if they accept my reasoning – but I expect to go on enquiring into the movements, motives and characters of everybody concerned. So stick around, Mr Hooper, and we'll start with a few questions for you.'

'And until you've caught somebody, Tim is in danger?' Ann asked.

'We have to recognize it as a possibility.'

'You do realize,' Tim said, 'that I knew nothing about you being an heiress until this moment?'

'Of course, silly,' Ann said, laughing. 'If it bothers you, I'll put advertisements in all the papers, saying just that. And on telly. I can quite see that you wouldn't want it thought that you were after my money.' She broke off and put a hand to her mouth. 'Gosh, it does feel funny saying that. I never before had any money worth anybody being after. What Brionie was working towards was that as soon as we're married and I've made my will leaving everything to my dear husband, there will be no more danger. Isn't that right?'

'Almost,' said Brionie. 'Discounting the possibility of a plot against each of you, together or separately, yes. To that, add the fact that a family wedding would be ideal for drawing the family members out of the woodwork. How quickly could we set it up?'

'Hadn't we better decide where we want to live?' Tim suggested.

Ann considered the question for a microsecond. 'I don't have a house,' she said. 'Uncle Gus had a flat at the top of Dingle's but I wouldn't want to live there and Umber would hate it. I'll move in with you, if you'll have me.'

Mr Headstone coughed to bring everyone to order. 'First,' he said, 'we had better see about signing an interim will, just in case. Thereafter, leave it to me.'

The wedding was put together with haste not generally expected when the bride is *virgo intacta;* and most unusual in Scotland where special licenses do not exist. In this they were greatly aided by the services of Mr Headstone and by the results of a second scan of Tim's head. This revealed that his symptoms had been caused by a very small subdural haematoma which, now that it was large enough to be seen, could also be deemed not to require surgery but to be almost certain to yield to medication. Tim's release, after further tests, could be set for two days ahead after which he was agreeable to being treated as an outpatient. Ann said that she would need that interval to prepare the house, with the aid, she hoped, of the Occupational Therapy ladies, for receipt of the invalid.

In Scotland, the period of notice may be cut very short in special circumstances. They never knew what arguments Mr Headstone advanced but there was much trafficking by email and then by courier and the necessary permission was obtained.

The wedding itself took place in the hospital chapel on the day preceding Tim's return home, in the presence of a congregation comprising a few members of Ann's family, two of Tim's friends and any patients or staff members free and wishing to attend. The chapel was well filled.

The Reverend Downing objected strongly to taking the ceremony but his bishop, who was becoming rather tired of the Reverend's misbehavior, told him to shut up and get on with it. A female employee of Dingle's, temporarily hospitalized with a female complaint that was only referred to in whispers, turned out to be a regular stand-in church organist and gave good service. The bride wore her favorite yellow dress and carried a bouquet of late yellow roses. Detective Sergeant Brionie Phelps acted as bridesmaid and Ann's stepfather, under some pressure from his wife, gave her away.

They returned together along what there was of an aisle. Tim was leaning on the bride's arm – he had spent much time in bed or seated and, although the hospital staff had struggled to keep his legs working, he was stiff and weak. He was driven to whispering again. 'What's *he* doing here?'

Ann had no difficulty divining the subject of Tim's enquiry. Leo Fogle, gaunt as ever, was half a head taller than anyone else in the congregation. He seemed to have made some small effort. He had shaved and he was wearing a tie but he was still by far the scruffiest person present. 'Ignore him. Explanations later,' Ann replied. They paused for a moment outside the chapel where a photographer with a studio in Dingle's prepared to take photographs. They now had a moment of comparative privacy. 'He's a very remote cousin of mine,' Ann whispered. 'We could hardly shut him out. But we won't let anybody know that he's a relative. He has a problem.'

'A drug problem?' Brionie asked sharply from close behind them. 'He could need money.'

'He always seems to have some,' said Ann, 'I think he has an annuity or something.'

The photographer announced that he was ready.

The hospital matron or Senior Nursing Officer, a formidable battleaxe with a voice more suited to a Guards RSM, had turned out to have a soft heart. The hospital kitchen produced a masterpiece of a cake and a mountain of hors d'oeuvres. Aided by a cheque from the groom, several boxes of a quite respectable wine were obtained through the bride's stepfather, who had come to accept that Ann's legacy was passing beyond his reach but was prepared to settle for the smaller legacy to her mother. After the ceremony, those who were permitted alcohol retired into a room that had long before been a maternity ward but which had been withdrawn from service when Maternity was transferred to the Infirmary and, by sleight of constructive bookkeeping, retained for the use of staff and friends holding a weekly dance there. It was said that the room, by facilitating the courtships normal to the daily life of a hospital, was continuing to make an indirect contribution to its original purpose.

Bride and groom, meantime, withdrew to Tim's single-bed ward where it was overtly supposed that they were changing for 'going away'. Less openly it was quite understood that the brief interval might well be all the honeymoon that they could expect for the moment.

Ann was not so totally innocent that she did not understand where Tim's inclination was leading when he began very gently to disrobe them both. She had understood that a bed played a significant role in the post-nuptial celebrations but the single bed present in the ward seemed rather cramped for any such purpose.

'Trust me,' Tim said. With his artificial foot removed he leaned heavily on her shoulder but managed, while hopping, to steer her into the shower cubicle. He had already bespoken two shower caps.

'I do,' replied his bride. 'Absolutely.'

Whether or not their coupling was successful for each of them, information is sadly lacking. One can only draw inferences from the fact that Tim's headaches never made a return.

ELEVEN

Tim was returned home by Patient Transport, to find that his house had been given a new sparkle by an assault of Ann aided by two of her female relatives. The garden too was freshly dug over, the vegetable bed tidied and the patch of lawn weeded, rolled and given a last cut of the year. That much he could appreciate during a quick glance around while being tenderly helped from ambulance to bedroom. He gave a little sigh of satisfaction. Ann could never have accomplished so much unaided. It seemed that he had been absorbed into the community, despite his reclusive lifestyle. During his absence the frosts had visited and autumn colours had taken over in the gardens and trees. The neighbourhood was looking its best.

He had been sadly lacking in exercise since being struck down. His legs were too weak to allow long walks to enjoy the change of scenery, but he found Ann determined to have him back on his feet without unnecessary delay. With this in mind, she was feeding him generously and well. To this he had no objection, but he was plagued by physiotherapists similarly disposed, each one adamant that he must do exercises until long after exhaustion had set in. He considered writing a murder mystery in which a physiotherapist would be painfully killed by an exhausted patient, but such a tale had already been written by a writer of his acquaintance, who, Tim assumed, had suffered the similar attentions.

Umber, it need hardly be said, was ready to explode with joy at having her beloved master returned to her. ('Don't *lick* me, horrible dog,' Tim said fondly. 'I love you too but I don't lick you.' Umber only grinned and wagged her whole latter end.) Ann had coped well with

her training and upkeep and Umber, who seemed to understand that Tim was not yet fit for long walks, was happy
to accompany her new mistress, but whenever Tim was
at his desk or in his dining chair Umber was likely to be
sprawled beside him with her head weighing heavily on
his foot.

They settled into a new routine. In between periods of
exercise, Tim sat at his desk, working on his new novel
or sometimes just daydreaming of the rich change that
had come over his life. In the evenings the television was
abandoned unless there was something special to be
viewed and instead they would sit at the computer, secure
against the encroaching dark outside, reading over and
discussing what he had written that day. Ann's comments
were shyly given but always to the point.

More than a week went past. They had almost forgotten
the attack on Tim, whose efforts to regain his legs had
progressed from the Zimmer frame via two sticks to a
single stick. He was managing short walks with his two
companions though Ann had to walk Umber again to
make up the total mileage required by a Labrador. Ann
had taken to marital games as though she had invented
them but when she managed to provoke Tim into pursuing
her around the house with amorous intent and much
giggling she had at first to invent special excuses to slow
her pace; but now it seemed that he might soon be able
to catch her without any such concession. He was looking
forward to that prospect and planning each delicious move
while watching Ann from a window as she planted out
a batch of seedlings from the garden centre. The weather
was perfect, drizzling. For pricking out seedlings, drizzle
is perfection.

A medium sized Ford in blue and white livery passed
through his field of view, preparing to pull up at his door.
For Tim, this was a sudden awakening from what had
become a dream of sensual delight alternating with harmo-
nious work. Questions of assault on his person had been
relegated to a remote corner of his mind but they soon

came flooding back. He opened his front door as Brionie
Phelps, in uniform again, got up out of the driver's seat
and walked around the front of the car, carrying a heavy
briefcase. She opened the passenger's door for a stout,
florid-faced man in a stiff blue suit and a nylon rain-
coat.

Tim, in his innocence, was surprised that a man should
expect or even accept such respectful treatment from an
attractive young lady. He could well imagine that there
would be a tug-of-war between courtesy and discipline
in the police force. In the unlikely event of his ever being
caught up in such a conflict he hoped that good, old fash-
ioned manners would triumph. Perhaps to make this point,
he shook the newcomer's hand when Brionie introduced
him as Detective Inspector Powell and then gave Brionie
an identical greeting. He knew that the point had been
taken without knowing quite how he knew it. Perhaps
there had been a slight stiffening of the DI's already
ramrod spine or a curl of a supercilious lip.

'Shall I call my wife?' Tim asked.

'Not yet,' said Powell coldly. 'Let's hear what you have
to say first.'

Tim led them into his sitting room and gave them
seats. The room was very comfortable and cheerfully
furnished. The background warmth furnished by the
central heating was supplemented by the log fire that Tim
had lit to ward off the chill of approaching winter, but
there was no relaxation in the room. It was soon clear to
Tim that Powell was of a mindset that he had met and
loathed elsewhere – the senior who boosts his own ego
or status by diminishing those of his subordinates. He
made Brionie explain her investigation up to the time of
the wedding and demanded that Tim confirm or deny
almost every point. Brionie's attempts to analyse and elim-
inate various accidental means by which he might have
been struck down seemed to call for particular ridicule.
Tim could see that Brionie was beginning to seethe but
he knew that his interference would only make bad worse.

He also realized that Brionie, now that she was challenged, was emerging as an efficient and lucid officer.

'And you encouraged this . . . proceeding?' Powell demanded, referring to the wedding.

'I went along with it.'

'Despite the effect that it would have on the obtaining of evidence?'

Brionie spoke up in a choked voice. She had been pushed to the verge of explosion. 'I had no grounds for stopping it. If you are referring to the fact that a wife can not be compelled to give evidence against her husband—'

'I am.'

'I could see no way that Mr Russell could or would have inflicted that injury on himself. And since it was patently obvious that she was deeply in love with him there would not have been the least chance of her testifying against him even if she had known him for the Antichrist. On the other hand, the marriage seemed to offer the best guarantee of his survival. His murder would have left us with one more crime and one fewer witness.'

'It would certainly have produced more evidence.'

Brionie drew a long breath through her teeth. 'Mr Powell,' she said, 'I would advise you not to make that argument to anyone in the higher ranks.'

The detective inspector seemed about to ask why not but he realized in time how it would look if he should ever admit considering one murder to be an acceptable trade for the faint possibility of more evidence about an unsuccessful attempt at a different one. He changed tack. 'And you are such an experienced judge of loving couples?'

There was a silence. Powell clearly knew that each passing second would exacerbate Brionie's difficulty in making an acceptable reply. At last she decided to be jocular. 'I have had my moments,' she said.

Powell stared at her for a few long seconds before deciding to let the remark fall flat. 'When it was agreed that the marriage would take place,' he said, 'and as soon as the present Mrs Russell knew that she had the legacy coming, the man Hooper, the bride's stepfather, tried to leave; but you told him to stay and make a statement. What did you find out at that time?'

Brionie opened the fat briefcase and took out what appeared to be a typed and signed statement together with many pages of untidy shorthand notes. 'Mr Hooper was evasive and uncommunicative. He admitted that he had no alibi for that time. I only learned anything else of interest in a second interview, two days later. Do you want the outcome of both interviews?'

Mr Powell looked at her as though she had farted. 'Of course. Why wouldn't I?'

'Because you asked me what I found out *at that time*.'

Powell bristled. Tim guessed that he was looking for some offence that he could latch onto but was finding none. What Brionie had said was a precise and obedient response to his order made in the presence of a witness. Tim tried not to smile but he probably exuded amusement.

Brionie offered her senior a quick face-saver by speaking on. 'In the first interview he denied knowing anything of the legacy before Mrs Russell – Ann – was advised of it in his presence by the solicitor, Mr Headstone. At the second interview I was able to tell him truthfully that other witnesses had stated and were prepared to testify that he knew about it earlier – just before his visit to this house, in fact. He had been told of it by Mrs Hooper as she still is and they discussed the implications of any romance between the present Mr and Mrs Russell. I can give you a word for word account of our interview if you wish but I can say that he absolutely and categorically denies that there was any discussion of scotching such a romance or of an attack on Mr Russell and he denies even more vehemently having carried out that attack.'

'That's a bit rich,' Tim said. 'When he came here he tried to pretend that Ann was under age and he said that he'd come to take her back. We can guess why.'

Powell switched his disdainful air to Tim. 'Yes, yes,' he said. 'You are already on record with that statement.'

'And when I confronted him with it,' said Brionie, 'he first tried to call you a liar until I read out that portion of Mrs Russell's statement. Then he turned about and pretended that he'd misunderstood both the situation and the question. His visit, he said, had been intended to rescue his stepdaughter from the clutches of one who he believed at the time to be a potentially bad moral influence on her. He expressed himself delighted with the marriage and again absolutely denied that any suggestion that Mr Russell be attacked had ever been made to him, by him or in his presence.

'I then told him the details that he denied already knowing, that Mr Russell had been found lying face down in the mud with a wound in his head by a witness who had seen him alone and on his feet only very few seconds earlier and I asked him how he thought that such an end could have been contrived. He seemed to have been expecting the question. I concluded that if he had committed the assault it had not been by the means he suggested.'

Powell, who had begun to lose interest in what was, after all, a reiteration of the story, sat up suddenly. 'Why do you say that?' he demanded.

'His answer came immediately without his having to think about it . . . and too quickly for him to be the guilty party. His suggestion was so unlikely that if it had described an act that he had committed he would not have blurted it out so unhesitatingly, but I could very well understand a man, confronted with such a mystery, turning over conceivable explanations in his head, adjusting them to take account of every anomaly until he arrived at a . . . a scenario that fitted with that Sherlock Holmes adage about what ever remained, however unlikely, having to be the truth. He started from the fact that only stones were lying around in the garden or in the field. He could not suggest a means of projecting a stone with the necessary energy and had concluded that there had been some other projectile. His solution was an icicle made in a deep freeze and fired from a muzzle-loading firearm. I pointed out that no sound of a shot had been heard and that none of Mrs Russell's relatives appeared to own any antique weapons.'

There was a pause while Brionie searched through the detached pages of shorthand. 'Ah! Here it is. He replied that the late Mr Tirrell had not been averse to doing a deal occasionally or to taking valuables in settlement of a bad debt and had in consequence owned several. I said that I had never heard of a muzzle-loader being fitted with a sound moderator and he pointed out that that did not mean that it had never happened.

'As soon as I had his statement down in pale grey and white – I never knew an economy drive go down as far as printer and typewriter ribbons and carbon paper before . . .'

'Get on with it, girl,' Powell snapped. 'You're not here to criticize the management of the Force's budgets.'

Brionie, having made her point, resumed. 'I hurried to Dingle's and had Mr Tirrell's secretary let me into his private flat and into the strong room that was used for valuables, money and firearms. It's a bit of an Aladdin's cave. It seems that a number of reputedly better-heeled locals who didn't want to lose face with the townsfolk had been trading in paintings, silver or china against their necessities. Mr Tirrell had, in fact, been acting as an informal and unlicensed pawnbroker. Mr Headstone will have to get busy obtaining valuations, but that's another matter.

'And here we come to the point at which a highly improbable theory begins to look faintly possible. There were a number of muzzle-loaders there, five of them, mostly long guns but one of them a pistol. The secretary said that that was funny, she could have sworn that there were two pistols.'

The detective inspector, who had seemed about to doze off, sat up quickly. 'One is missing?'

'It seems so, if the secretary's recollection is correct. As it happens,' Brionie admitted shyly, 'I had a boyfriend who was into antique guns. He dragged me along to the National Championships once and made me compete. In fact, I shot rather well, which I think is what doomed that particular romance. That's how I came to notice that Mr Tirrell's guns were all flintlock. Pebble and steel, you know? Well, that's unusual. There was a period before cartridges and breech-loading came into general use when percussion caps took over and they worked so much more reliably than flintlocks that most surviving flintlocks were converted. But the collector who had traded in his collection, along with a tin of black powder, against a year's supply of fine wines, mostly Champagne, had not been interested in what he regarded as a twenty-year passing fad. The flintlock had two hundred years of history during which almost every feature of the modern gun evolved.

'But that's by the way. The remaining pistol was a large horse-pistol which I could well imagine propelling an icicle, but the secretary was quite sure that if there ever had been another pistol it too had been flintlock. What's more, the secretary was adamant that the other pistol had been much smaller, and at that point, as far as I was concerned, that theory went out of the window.'

DI Powell, who had been looking stunned by this flood of information, roused himself enough to raise his eyebrows and to make an interrogatory noise resembling that of a gorilla disturbed in its nest.

'The flash,' Brionie explained. 'If the pistol was fitted with a noise attenuator – a silencer – that would diminish the muzzle-flash in daylight almost to nothing, but this event took place in the dusk and the flash of a flintlock, which has an external flash pan, would have lit up the whole area.'

Mr Powell frowned loftily. 'You're saying that Mrs Russell – Miss Erskine as she was then – at the kitchen window could hardly have failed to see the flash?'

'I am also saying that nobody with a view of the outdoors for a hundred metres around could have missed it. But to close off that line of argument I made two other enquiries. Firstly, with the exception of the dealer, Mr Waller, our suspects so far are relatives of Mrs Russell or friends of those relatives and therefore of the late Mr Tirrell. They seem to have one and all been in the habit of visiting him to ask for discounts or extended credit or other favours. Each of them would have known that his flat was usually unlocked all day and that the strong room keys were kept in a desk drawer. On the other hand, icicles have been used as projectiles often in works of fiction but I wondered whether anyone had ever checked experimentally that it was possible. I consulted my friends at the university. They were of the opinion that the combined heat of the propellant plus the friction with the air would melt the projectile before it had gone more than a metre or two.

'But no academic can ever be confronted with a puzzle and be satisfied with a mathematical solution – they have to have the empirical experiment as well. So I was then dragged to the university's rifle range and kept standing in an icy wind while they proved it. To make assurance doubly sure, they wanted me to stand and have icicles fired at me from varying distances but at that point I chickened out.'

After a delay that seemed filled with unuttered arguments, DI Powell spoke up. 'You seem to have eliminated that particular suspect using that particular method,' he said, 'but I feel that you've been just a bit credulous. Does it not occur to you that the suspect, finding himself confronted by a young and gullible officer, might have decided to pull the wool over her eyes, distracting her from how he had in reality committed the deed? You had better take another look at Mr Hooper, my girl, and not let your judgement be clouded by all the masculinity and sex appeal.'

If Mr Powell's intention was to push Brionie to the point of open rebellion it was evident that he was coming close to success. Rather than allow a jealous man to wreck a young woman's career on a whim, Tim decided that a technical argument might keep the debate alive with the opponents brought onto the same side. Besides, he disliked Mr Hooper. 'There's one other possibility,' he said. 'I've heard that a functional silencer can be contrived using a plastic cola bottle and sticky tape. If one of the darkened bottles were used it might also suppress the flash from the muzzle.'

Immediately, he felt himself to be the focus of twin contemptuous stares. The DI said, 'That would still leave a bright flash from the flash pan.'

And Brionie said, 'At dusk, the muzzle-flash can reach out as much as two metres, the height of a tall man. I've seen it. I can't imagine a bottle hiding that.' The two officers looked at each other in a moment of sympathy. These interfering members of the public might be trying to be helpful but . . .

'Sorry I spoke,' Tim said.

'All the same,' Powell said mildly. 'It's the kind of suggestion that defence counsel might produce. It would be wise to disprove it. That's for your attention, Sergeant. And now I think we should see Mrs Russell. Perhaps you would invite her to come down to the station with us.'

It was another occasion for Brionie to argue. Tim's attention was wandering. The significance of Brionie's statement that Ann was deeply in love with him was only now surfacing. Until then he had looked on their relationship as being compounded out of friendship, humour and sexual desire, which combination he had regarded as a propitious basis for marriage – a base from which love could be expected to grow. Now that his selfish and wayward attention was drawn to it, he realized that, by all the signs, Brionie was correct. If Ann were suddenly to disappear from his life . . .

But there was a prior claim to his attention. He said, 'I insist on my right to be present when you question my wife.'

'So be it,' said the DI. Tim decided that he was confusing himself with God. Not an easy mistake to make.

TWELVE

Ann had finished pricking out the box of seedlings and could be heard upstairs, showering and getting more suitably dressed. She had divined that this was no occasion for jeans. It took only a call from Brionie to bring her down, neat and shining in one of her new dresses. Tim thought that the sitting room which, on such a dull day, seemed very dark, was brighter for her arrival; but that may have been because her first act was to switch on the wall brackets. Her second was to give Tim a quick kiss on the cheek. She knelt and put a log on the log fire already glowing in the fireplace, sending a cloud of sparks up the chimney, before settling neatly into a tapestry fireside chair.

'Your husband,' the DI began, 'insists on being present while you are questioned. Have you any objection?' His tone suggested that an objection might be quite understandable. Any question of removal to the police station seemed to have gone by the board for the moment.

Ann laughed. 'Of course not. Why would I?'

'We shall see. My sergeant seemed to accept that you're guiltless of the assault on your husband because of the evident affection in which you held him.'

Tim decided that as the intended victim he was the one person who could afford to attract the DI's hostility. 'And . . .' he said.

'I beg your pardon?'

'I was just reminding you that there are other and stronger reasons for believing in her innocence.'

'And may I remind you, Mr Russell, that you are only here as an observer.'

'I don't recall anything being said about my being only an observer. I insisted on being present to protect my wife's interests and if you seem to be stepping over the line, or if you try to exclude me, I'll halt the interview and call in a solicitor.'

'Your idea of the line may not coincide with mine.'

Tim decided that the DI was coming nicely to the boil. 'In that eventuality,' Tim said, 'my idea will prevail.' He returned most of his mind to the assertion that Ann loved him. He thought that you could trust one woman to read another.

DI Powell only nodded but his eyes were hot needles. 'Mrs Russell, according to the statement you gave my sergeant you were at the kitchen window and, looking out, you saw your husband at work in the garden. Seconds later you looked out again and saw him lying face down in the mud. Is that essentially correct?'

Ann, wide-eyed, nodded.

'That appears to be an affirmative answer. How many seconds later would you say?'

Ann closed her eyes and could be seen, from the tiny movements of her head, to be counting. 'Ten.' She said. 'Very approximately.'

'You can't have got much work done if you were looking out every ten seconds.'

Ann refused to be cowed. Her firm reply was worthy of a more mature woman. 'I wasn't looking out every ten seconds. Please don't put words in my mouth, Inspector. Some details have been coming back to me. I had just poured the water off some vegetables. I decided to finish my pastry-making before calling him. I paused and looked out again because my attention was caught – I think by a sound but it might have been a movement seen out of the corner of my eye.'

Tim would have been hard put to it to decide whether the inspector's glare was angry, contemptuous or challenging, or even all three, but it shifted to him. 'Mr Russell, would you agree with that estimate?'

'Yes.'

'But how do you know that you and your wife are

talking about the same interval between the same sight-
ings of each other?'

'Inspector,' Tim said, 'I was becoming hungry. I glanced
towards the kitchen window and saw that Ann was pouring
water from a saucepan, which is usually a good indication that a meal will soon be on the table. This was the
beginning of a new train of thought. I was wondering how
long the rest of that spit would take me and whether Ann
and my meal would wait that long. My best guess at the
time that I passed in musing on that topic before I seemed
suddenly to come to in the hospital would be five to fifteen
seconds. I have become quite sure that there is no memory
missing and the doctors in the hospital agreed.'

'Even if that's correct, it is still a guess and a very
approximate one,' Inspector Powell suggested. 'You weren't
thinking about the passing of time and you must have
noticed how time can slip away when you're cogitating?'

'I have noticed how time can slip away, but in this
instance I was in fact thinking about that very subject,
so I don't think that any extra time could have slipped
by unnoticed. Certainly not long enough for my wife, as
she is now, to have found or collected some tool, dashed
outside and whacked me over the head. That is, if she'd
wanted to do any such thing. I suppose that that's the
way your mind's working; I can't imagine any other
reason for your interest in the interval between her seeing
me at work and my being struck.'

Ann's face and knuckles were white. 'Nothing could
have been further from my mind. I had fallen hopelessly
in love,' she said bravely, 'and I knew it. So far from
wanting to hurt him, if I had seen anybody sneaking up
on him with a weapon I would happily have thrown
myself in between them and taken the blow myself. I
was in that sort of mood.' She paused and the colour
made a sudden return to her cheeks. 'As a matter of fact
I still am.'

This was more than Tim could bear. Love was a word
that was venerated by the young and treated with jocularity

by their elders but it had suddenly assumed reality. He turned towards her. 'Oh, my darling . . .'

There would have been no doubting the sincerity of either of them. The air between them seemed filled with a whole spectrum of emotions, ranging from an almost Victorian sentimentality to lust worthy of a pornographic video. For a moment the presence of two police officers had faded from their attention and if they had been left uninterrupted they might have given an unsolicited demonstration and proof of their affection right there on the hearthrug. Brionie Phelps, who was a sentimentalist at heart, was moved almost to tears.

Detective Inspector Powell, however, was clearly revolted. He was too adult and too concerned with his own dignity to resort to any childish miming of nausea but the impulse was there. 'Could you perhaps save these outbursts of affection for a more suitable occasion? I want to ask Mrs Russell about some of the other persons involved, particularly those who might have gained by her inheritance if she had died without being influenced by an affair of the heart. Their presence at your wedding would seem to be enough of an indicator. What, for instance, was that extraordinarily scruffy man doing there? Bogle, or some such name.'

'Leo Fogle? I wondered the same thing,' Tim said. He chose his words with care. 'He's a neighbour here but he certainly wasn't one of my wedding guests. At the conclusion of the wedding I learned that he is a remote cousin of my wife's. Neither of us has any idea who invited him. But there were some patients there as guests. I don't know that he was a patient either.'

'I don't know who invited him,' Ann said, 'but, as you say, he's a very remote relative of mine – third or fourth cousin at the closest – so I suppose somebody must have mentioned it to him. That would be quite enough to explain his being there. He's a bit of a sad case, really. When I was young, he was welcome in the family. He used to visit my parents – I think that both of his were dead, so mine felt that they had to try to give what little help they could. He was always friendly and seemed quite well behaved, just too nervous to look good in company. He has intelligence and education but he dropped out of university when he contracted a drug habit. It all happened when I was still young, just starting at school, but it's etched into my memory because of the fuss in the family. I think he'd stolen and altered a cheque, or something like that. I didn't understand the ins and outs of it at the time, but I think that the family got up a subscription and that Mr Tirrell put up most of the money. It was spent on putting Leo through a . . . a rehab clinic I suppose you'd call it and an eye was kept on him for several years afterwards. In fact, that's how I came to know about that place where you found me,' she said to Tim, 'from being sent out to play while my father was looking in on him.

'That was years ago but he seems to have spent the rest of his life fighting it. I respect him for that. He has a tiny income of his own and he sometimes gets short periods of work as a stand-in for postmen or people like that at busy times or when they go away on holiday. Mostly he just keeps himself to himself. He's very retiring, rather stand-offish or just plain shy.'

'I can't add anything to that,' said Tim. 'He lives in the second house to the right of here, the very small one adjoining the gate to the farmland, but I don't know him, not as you and I would interpret the word *know*. I don't think I've exchanged more than a dozen words with him altogether.'

The inspector said something that sounded very much like '*Humph!*' He stared into space for a long moment and then focused on Tim again. 'You might not be alarmed if your wife approached you quietly from behind.'

'That much at least is true,' Tim said.

'But I can imagine you spinning round defensively if, for instance, Mr Hooper seemed to be creeping up on you.'

'Or Woodworm Waller,' said Brionie.

'You've already mentioned him. Tell me more about him later. But, how would you have reacted if your new mother-in-law had approached you? Remember, she wasn't your mother-in-law at that time, she was the mother of the young girl on whom you were generally believed to have a bad influence.'

'Nobody could be afraid of my mother,' Ann said stoutly. 'She's a very gentle person. Of course, anybody can be made angry; but as far as she's concerned men are not the enemy, men only exist to protect her and solve all her problems for her.' She gave a small chuckle. 'I only realized that her attitude was rubbing off on me when the chain came off my bicycle and I found myself looking around for the nearest man to fix it. That's when I made up my mind to learn how to do things. I'm not a feminist but I'd be ashamed to have to run to a man for help with something that I could perfectly well have done for myself. Anyway, where would she have found a weapon? Or either of us, for that matter? Your questions still seem to be slanted in my direction.'

The inspector decided to ignore her challenge. Under the influence of the comfortable room and the firelight he was allowing a more conversational rather than inquisitorial air to prevail. 'I'll explain something,' he said. 'Imagine for a moment that you have a head that has come off a hammer and the handle is lost. You pick up that hammerhead in your fist and try to hammer in a nail or to knock somebody unconscious and you'll find it very difficult. Put it back on the handle and it will become much more effective. Now, instead of a hammerhead make it a heavy metal lump that won't be fitted onto a handle. Held in the hand it will be just as awkward. Drop it into a sock and you have a nasty and dangerous weapon.

'Now continue to imagine. You are approaching the home of somebody you hate or fear or from whom you have . . . expectations. You see that he is in his back garden, digging. Dusk is advancing, curtains are drawn and nobody seems to be looking out. Male or female, you can produce a long sock or a stocking – or with slightly more risk of attracting attention, tights. Drop a fist-sized stone into the toe and you have your weapon. Afterwards, discard the stone anywhere, wash out the sock or throw it away and,' said the inspector with an unaccustomed outburst of jocularity, 'Bob is no longer your uncle.'

Out of a silence Tim said, 'And you think that's what happened?'

The inspector's more customary morose attitude made a quick return. 'As every other theory proves to be a non-starter, that one begins to seem probable. Probable, but very difficult to prove against any individual. Would you say that twenty seconds was very approximately ten seconds?'

The sudden question was addressed to empty space. Tim decided to appropriate it. 'It's twice as much,' he said.

'But still within the bounds of *approximately*,' the inspector retorted. He pushed back his sleeve and fixed his eyes on a chromed wristwatch. 'Let's just see how long it is.' When Tim tried to speak, Powell held up a hand for silence. After a long pause he said, 'There. That was twenty seconds. Wouldn't you say that that was long enough for Mrs Russell to get out of the kitchen and arrive quietly behind her husband?'

Tim felt an upsurge of anger but nothing would be gained by losing his temper. Ann was visibly nearing flashpoint so Tim spoke quickly. 'That's a simple trick for making time seem longer. Waiting in silence and inactivity makes time drag by very slowly. Twenty seconds,' he said, 'or even ten, would be enough for anybody to approach from the corner of the house, or for something to fall from the sky, for God to smite me for my many naughtinesses or for Martians to land. It would have been long enough for you, Inspector, to have arrived and struck me down.'

'At that time, Mr Russell, I did not even know that you existed.'

Ann jumped in before Tim could spoil the effect. 'At that time, Inspector, you had just as much motive as I had, because I had none at all.'

Brionie just failed to suppress a tiny snort of laughter but Detective Inspector Powell was unmoved. He looked at the carriage clock over the mantelpiece. 'We may have to return to that topic later, Mrs Russell. For the moment, your comments on your family members and their contacts are illuminating. However, I am due at a meeting in HQ very shortly. You can both make yourselves available tomorrow morning?' It was barely a question.

Tim raised his eyebrows at Ann, who frowned but nodded. 'I suppose so,' he said.

'I'll send a car for you. Sergeant, you continue here. You know what's needed.'

He heaved himself to his feet and held out a hand for the car keys. When he had gone the atmosphere brightened as though clouds had blown away. Brionie sighed. 'I'm afraid I do know exactly what's needed,' she said. 'Endless attempts to catch your neighbours at home, to ask what if anything they saw. Nobody saw anything, of course, but the questions have to be asked.'

'Have a snack lunch with us,' Ann said. 'We can at least try to help by telling you at what times you're most likely to find each house occupied. We may not have met all our neighbours but at least we've seen them coming and going.'

'I'd love to,' said Brionie. 'According to the rules, written and unwritten, I should either accept a cup of tea and a biscuit and make do with that or go out to the nearest pub or café and accept what's cheapest on the menu. Well, they can forget about that. I have a healthy appetite and no shame about scrounging a meal.'

'If you're invited,' Tim said, 'it can't be called scrounging.'

'It can certainly be called scrounging,' Brionie said. 'It wouldn't be true but we have professional nit-pickers who can find a black side to anything.'

THIRTEEN

A small but highly polished panda car driven by a small female officer even younger than Brionie arrived to collect them while they were still taking their comparatively early breakfast. Tim refused to be hurried. The realization that their overpowering sexual attraction for each other was rooted in what could only be thought of as love – there was no other, less misused word for it – had lent a fresh urgency to his love-making and in the morning they were languorous. Tim had been afraid that his sedentary lifestyle allied to Ann's cooking was causing him to put on weight but now he began to fear that he might soon be wasting away through an excess of sex. Well, there were worse ways to slim. The inspector, he decided, was trying to show them how unimportant they were; but by revealing the need to impress them he was emphasizing their importance – as witnesses or suspects, they could not tell. The couple finished their breakfast and Tim washed the breakfast dishes while Ann gave Umber a shortened version of that vital morning walk. The young officer, who clearly lived in dread of the inspector, was nearly wetting herself by the time that they consented to be hustled into the car after giving Umber a lecture about behaviour in their absence. In consideration of his longer legs and their stiffness, Ann insisted that Tim be given the front seat. The car set off at speed but driven competently. Tim thought that the driver would have used sirens and flashing lights had the car been fitted with them.

Police HQ for that part of the county proved to be a modern building, well designed but already showing the stains to which lower cost materials are prone. They were ushered to an interview room with a view over both roofs

and countryside and abandoned there. It was Tim's habit,
however, always to carry a notebook and a supply of pens
and so when Detective Inspector Powell arrived there,
after a delay carefully calculated to induce a sense of
vulnerability, he found them with their heads close
together, concocting a mildly salacious love scene for the
conclusion of Tim's current novel. To his amazement he
found that they expected him to await their attention and
this he was forced to do for several minutes while, splut-
tering with laughter, they determinedly ignored his every
effort to break into their discussion and bandied between
them sentences that he would have hesitated to exchange
with his own wife. The utmost that he managed was to
avoid being drawn into their discussion.

When at last he had them seated around a table, with
Brionie Phelps taking notes and two tape recorders and
a video camera rolling, the inspector was at last able to
open the interview. 'I saw Mrs Hooper yesterday,' he told
Ann. 'Your mother. She was not a great deal of help. She
spent much of yesterday afternoon answering the questions that I hadn't asked and then seeking my advice on
points of law and almost anything else.'

'That does sound like my mother,' Ann admitted.

'She asked me to balance her chequebook,' the inspector
said indignantly. 'But never mind that. She claimed that
she had not the faintest idea where she was at the time
of the attack. And she could not think of anybody who
could do such a thing. Is she always so vague?'

'I'm afraid that she is,' Ann said. 'She always was.
When I was at school, I think that I came under an unusually good headmaster. Most of the others hated him, but
even at the time I recognized that his aim was not to stuff
me full of facts but to teach me to think for myself and
to learn without being spoon-fed. I think there must have
been a big change in Scottish schools in recent years.
My mother and many of her friends were at small, rural
schools and I've noticed that, just like many of her contem-
poraries, she's a red hot speller and her arithmetic's very

good, but her idea of geography stops short at the Tweed.
She has a fairly clear mental picture of heaven and hell,
although she has never managed to convey it to me, but
not the least idea of how the universe is put together. She
could list the names and birth dates of anybody related
to her, but if she's asked any other question she'd rather
ask the nearest man for the answer than trouble her mind
to think it out for herself.' Ann smiled wryly. 'I'm sorry
to have to speak about my own mother in that way, but
I can't have you thinking that she has something guilty
to hide. What you're seeing is all there is. She was a
good mother to me and a good housekeeper within the
limits of what was drummed into her, and she has a loving
nature and the softest heart in the world. I can quite see
why Dad married her but I can also see how she came
to drive him round the twist at times.'

The two men had listened to this speech in both patience
and awe – her husband startled by such mature observation in one so young while the policeman was impressed
to find his thoughts echoed and confirmed, unasked, in
such a quarter. 'You needn't go on,' Powell said. 'That's
much the picture that I already had of her. Of course,
even the most placid people can be pushed too far at
times.'

'Not my mum,' Ann said. 'Even if it wasn't against
her nature, she had no reason to attack Tim. She had
never met him. And she had nothing whatever to gain.
Even if she knew about my legacy at the time, which
you'll never get a clear answer on, and whether I was
married or single, she wouldn't expect a generous settlement from me. We – meaning she and I – both know that
she'd only surrender it to the next man who made up to
her. I've discussed it with Tim and we're agreed. We'll
make her an allowance. Anyway, money worries never
concern my mum. She never usually thinks about it. What
she needs she spends and there's always a man to pay
the bills. But it never amounts to very much. She doesn't
buy things for herself, she just waits for a man to bring

her presents. The only way she's extravagant is, for instance, if she sees a lame dog or a picture of a starving child; then she's in tears and wants to do something for every child or to feed every dog in the world. I can sympathize with that even if I wouldn't let her go overboard trying. Am I making sense?'

'A whole lot of sense,' Tim assured her.

'When I asked her how you, Mr Russell, came by the wound,' Inspector Powell said, 'she tried to tell me at first that you must have walked into something. We took her to your garden and when she saw that there was nothing there that you could have hit your head on she suggested something falling from an aeroplane. "Coming unscrewed", she said. That sounds daft, but ice does form on aircraft and fall off when de-icers are switched on and, very occasionally, nuts do come unscrewed and fall to earth. The trouble with that is that the authorities are adamant that there were no planes over here at that time and the sergeant here has asked all your neighbours and they're unanimous in insisting that there was no sound of a plane.'

'So we're back with the brick-in-a-sock theory?' Tim said.

Ann's unaccustomed verbosity seemed to have found an echo in the inspector. 'Until somebody comes up with a better suggestion. Proper investigation would be to concentrate on how the deed was done, which will nearly always lead to who did it. In this case we must go on trying to figure out just that. You may have noticed that officers in overalls have been going through the rubbish bins?' (Ann and Tim looked blank.) 'No? Somebody may have tried to dispose of a sock or stocking; and if we find such a thing it may point to its original wearer. There may have been attempts to wash it, but blood is much more difficult to remove than is generally realized. If that produces nothing, as it may well do, with luck one of the team will say a word that suggests the only possible truth and we'll all say "of course, how obvious!" But just in case that useful person is still twenty years off, we must look at people. Sergeant Phelps has given me an outline of your fight with "Woodworm" Waller. Now it's your turn to tell me all about it.' When Tim hesitated, Powell went on, 'I have no intention of prosecuting you for not reporting a punch-up some days old in which nobody was seriously hurt. If Waller suddenly drops dead of a delayed clot on the brain it might be different, but perhaps not by very much.'

'On that understanding, then,' Tim began. At his invitation, Ann told the story of how she had been tricked out of her due. Tim had to choke her off when, with her eyes shining, she began an enthusiastic account of Tim's confrontation with the dealer, miming an account of most of the action. He explained his own knowledge of martial arts and then gave a more subdued account of the battle.

'Waller has never made a complaint to us,' said the inspector, 'which suggests that he did not feel that right was on his side. I can understand your motivation for keeping quiet about it yourself, but if only you had complained about your books at the time we might have brought a case that would have put him out of business. What was your opinion of his intelligence?'

'Not very high. He has enough cunning to buy and sell, but that's about his limit. Any kind of trouble he'll meet with his fists.' Tim paused and then decided that the subject was better out in the open. 'Inspector, if your thoughts are drifting in the direction of Waller being angry enough to come after me for having duffed him up and recovered what Ann and I were due, there may well be something in it. I would put him down as not being bright enough to see that he would gain nothing and risk a lot by looking for revenge. But if you take any action do please bear in mind that for some weeks yet I may be suffering from more than one disability, and Waller probably knows it. Don't put me at risk any more than you must. I do not know any defensive moves available to the cripple that do not entail killing or very seriously injuring his attacker, so please be warned.'

The inspector only nodded, but from their moment of eye contact Tim was suddenly aware of him as being more astute than Tim had so far given him credit for. Powell might have his quirks but he did not lack intelligence. 'I'll take as much care as I can,' the inspector said. 'In return, please restrain your lady wife from carrying a weapon. I am half tempted to egg Waller on to have a go at you in the hope of getting him out of my hair for ever, but I am bound by the spirit of the law. Also, I would not like to prosecute her.'

Tim gave urgent thought to this new subject and realized that he was thinking along a track parallel to that followed by the inspector seconds earlier. Ann would have seen that her husband was no longer so able to defend himself if attacked. She would see herself as his protector. But she was not skilled at fighting with bare hands and she had no weapon of her own. She could hardly hide any heavy stick or other potential club about her person although he had noticed that a cricket bat, no longer used, had moved from the hall cupboard to a place beside the front door. She had no access to a firearm. Or a sword . . . but a knife, now. He turned and held out his hand to her. 'Ann, give me the knife.'

She froze. He guessed that she was torn between lying to him or defying him. But loyalty won out. She bent forward, reached under her short skirt and came up with a knife that he recognized as being one of the kitchen set and very sharp.

'You'd better give me whatever you're using as a sheath.'

She shook her head and tapped her thigh. He realized that an improvised sheath taped to her thigh would be difficult to remove modestly. His mind took a sideways step for a moment as he realized that she had let him see her in a state of near nudity long before there had been any signs of an affair between them and yet she grudged the inspector a glimpse of her legs. Was this the feminine fear of arousing the male or did she now see herself as a married lady and therefore exclusive to one admirer? 'All right,' he said. 'You carry it home, very carefully. Then it goes back into the kitchen drawer. The law says that carrying a concealed weapon is a crime and that we must depend on Detective Inspector Powell to protect us.'

He thought that his own voice sounded as doubtful as Ann's expression but the knife vanished under the skirt. 'I'll accept that for the moment,' Powell said, 'but leave it in the kitchen drawer and never take it out except for culinary purposes. That means—'

'Cooking,' said Ann.

'Well, yes.' The inspector looked at her reprovingly. Young blondes had no right, in his view, to be familiar with long words or, if so literate, to admit to such erudition, thereby stealing his thunder. 'Try to be near a phone or carry a mobile and I'll arrange for a car to attend immediately if you call for help. That, sadly, is as far as I can go. Of course, the law can't forbid you ever to have a heavy stick within reach. A stick is not a weapon until you hit or threaten somebody with it.' With that strong hint he seemed to feel that the subject had been exhausted.

He was soon in the middle of questioning Ann about any possible connection between her family and Waller and receiving in return nothing but indignant denials. It appeared that members of the family had only sold discarded items to Waller when no other purchaser could be found and would under no circumstances have bought anything from him. The inspector was interrupted by the insistent ringing of a mobile phone. Brionie, who was in plain clothes once more, snatched her phone out of a doeskin handbag. She listened for a few seconds and passed the phone to DI Powell. Tim and Ann could hear a faint muttering but the caller's words were indistinguishable. After perhaps half a minute, during which the inspector's brows were drawn down into a petulant scowl, he disconnected and tapped a few words into the phone. Brionie scanned the short text and nodded. She got to her feet.

'The interview is over,' she said. 'I'll run you home.'

During the journey she was not to be drawn on what was afoot but they were left in no doubt that it was serious. 'What do you suppose that was about?' Tim said as soon as the front door had closed behind them.

'Whatever, it can't concern us,' Ann said. She considered nibbling his ear and then fleeing up the stairs, but it was still early in the day for that sort of thing. 'You have a seat at your desk and go on putting in the finishing touches,' she said. 'I'll take Umber out onto the grass.'

FOURTEEN

They were offered no explanation for the sudden end of the interview but they were becoming used to that kind of discourtesy from the police. They resumed what they hoped would be the normal course of life – writing, walking Umber and taking huge pleasure in their love. It was not until the afternoon of the following day that the story, which must have been carefully hidden or embargoed, broke.

Ann heard it first on the kitchen radio. She appeared at Tim's side but waited until he became aware of her presence. 'It just came over the news on the radio. A general dealer in this town – well, surely that couldn't be anyone but Woodworm Waller, could it?'

'That depends,' Tim said. 'What did he do?'

'Not a lot. His was a passive role. He was found dead in his shop, transfixed by an oriental dagger just like in the detective stories.'

Tim felt that this light-hearted approach to the death of an acquaintance, however hostile the acquaintance, ran contrary to respect for the forces of life; but he did not want to check her exuberance too directly. He decided on an oblique change of slant if not of subject. '*Trans* means through,' he said. 'A dagger would hardly be long enough to transfix somebody fatally. *Stabbed* would have been enough if a little less grandiose. And if it was the dagger that I saw hanging on the wall in his shop it was Turkish. Part of Turkey is in Europe so it hardly counts as an oriental dagger. Did they give any more details?'

Ann looked up at the ceiling in an effort of memory. 'It said that he was fifty-six. Well, they always tell people's ages, it's the easiest thing to find out. He was found yesterday midday by a customer, a woman who was looking for

dining chairs, and she's been taken to hospital, in shock.
She must be rather feeble if she collapses at the sight of
a body and a little blood, but some people have no moral
fibre. Subject to the pathologist's report, they're assuming
that he died yesterday morning, which means that he must
have still been warm when he was found. Anyone who
saw him or visited his shop yesterday is asked to contact
them. Which is a fat lot of good,' Ann added indignantly,
'if they haven't told us who it is. Or do you suppose that
it's a trap and only a guilty person could be sure who it
was?'

'I doubt that they're that subtle,' Tim said. 'Individuals
think like that but larger organizations get hidebound.
Middle-rankers get fed up, having it pointed out to them
that they've made a mistake. Some desk-bound copper
is probably having his nose rubbed in the fact that he's
asked the public to help without making it clear what
they're being asked to help with. Was that all?'

'It's all that I can remember. The rest was waffle. You
know how it is. Some hack journalist is sent out by his
editor and the police aren't saying a word more than they
want to, so he speaks to a few neighbours and fills up
the rest of the vacant space with speculation and background.'

Tim was nodding. He had noticed, and even admired,
the journalist's gift for making bricks without straw. 'How
right you are! And in the process he probably lands his
employers in a libel action by speculating a little too
much,' Tim said. He returned to his writing. His heroine
was turning from being a bit of a hard-nosed bitch towards
being a soft and sentimental airhead. Perhaps Ann would
be able to help him to toughen the character. On the other
hand, it was probably Ann's influence that was at the
root of the problem. Perhaps one person could exhibit
both characteristics. That might add depth. He made a
note to consider for his next book.

His words about libel were to return to haunt him. The
police issued no more statements for several days but

word of his fight with the late Mr Waller had reached the media, possibly, he thought, released in order to take pressure off the investigating officers. Several phone calls from editors did no more than open up the subject; it was the personal visit by a reporter with his subtly probing questions that was expected to flush out the drama. Would-be investigative journalists began to arrive at the door, determined not to leave until presented with some scurrilous titbit. He resisted the temptation to redirect them towards Mr Hooper, the Reverend Downing, Leo Fogle or even his mother-in-law. Any one of those might give the reporters a little too much information about him and Ann.

Sometimes the truth is the best evasion; but Tim could see that the bald facts of his fight with Woodworm Waller would only lead into endless speculation hesitating just disappointingly short of libel. Somehow the news hounds had failed to learn of the attempt on Tim's life. He and Ann both resorted to 'no comment' and stuck to it until the last cub reporter had given up and gone home for the night.

In this manner nearly a week went by. The police seemed to be avoiding them as though they had an especially contagious version of syphilis. The only news that they gleaned came from the unlikely source of a supermarket driver. Reporters were still lying in wait whenever nothing more immediate beckoned, so Ann and Tim had taken to doing their shopping by telephone and only walking Umber on those occasions when they could escape from the house unaccompanied. There was neither pleasure nor training to be attained in the midst of a group of reporters, each trying to assert his own question over those of his rivals.

The driver who delivered a full week's worth of edibles was full of his own importance. On the day of the murder he had been on a late shift and was at the depot's loading bay, almost opposite Waller's shop, waiting for the belated delivery of bread to complete his load. As he began his wait he saw Waller rearranging some china in the window of his shop. Unfortunately, during the wait while the bread arrived and individual orders were bagged, his attention had been directed towards the window of a TV shop beside the loading bay, where a drama was unfolding on the illuminated screens, so he had seen nothing of any comings or goings. Even without sound the action was largely unmistakable and this had formed a valuable check on the passing of time. Only as he was able at last to depart on his delivery round did he notice the arrival of the four-by-four pickup belonging to the husband of the lady who found the body.

With the time of death established to within a bracket of an hour or so, that hour happened to be at a time when the constables had arrived at the Russell house to take Tim and Ann down to the station the previous morning. There had followed some days of vacuum during which, they gathered when Brionie at last reappeared, Tim, as the only person known to have had a physical fight with the murdered dealer, had been a suspect and very definitely off Brionie's visiting list until his alibi, which seemed a little too good to be true, had been checked and rechecked, up, down and sideways.

'And,' Brionie said frankly, 'as long as you were a suspect my *bona fides* also were in question, so I was relegated to filing, collating and cross-checking until your innocence was accepted. Luckily one of your neighbours remembered seeing the police car outside your door for most of the critical period. Meanwhile it became officially a murder with a superintendent in charge; and the longer it goes unsolved the bigger the team will grow – within reason, of course. So now we're all falling over each other, spreading house-to-house enquiries ever further afield as other avenues become exhausted. And you may not have thought of yourselves as another avenue, but that's what you are. I'm to invite you to come to Waller's shop and tell us what you can detect that differs from the way the shop was when you had your disagreement with Waller.'

'That was some time ago,' Tim said. 'There could have been a lot of changes in a working shop since then.'

'I expect so. We're trying to build up a picture of who was in the shop and when.'

'You'd get the same information more easily from his books,' Ann said.

'It's the visits that don't appear in the books that we most want to know about. And yes, I know that it's likely to be a total waste of time but that's what detection is all about. You gather up a whole lot of facts and if even one of them turns out to be useful and if anybody notices that fact, then you've struck oil.' She sighed. 'I'll be just as interested to have a proper look. As I told you, I was shunted into a siding while my bosses thought that you might not be squeaky clean. I've only had a passing glimpse in there myself.'

An hour later Mr and Mrs Russell were back in the shop once belonging to the late Mr Waller. Umber was confined to the car.

'Just look around,' said Brionie. 'Don't touch anything but tell us if you notice anything different from the last time you were here.'

That was rather a tall order. Two men in plain clothes with clipboards were poking through the miscellanea of objects. They were accompanied by a woman in a smock who held one of Mr Waller's ledgers and was ticking off items as they were identified. The big front window was covered with some translucent material against the curiosity of passers-by, there was a screen inside the door and the whole place looked different in the unfamiliar mixture of artificial light with filtered daylight. A taped outline on the floor looked surprisingly small, considering the large man it represented. It was being ignored and already showed signs of much wear.

Some of the mountains of furniture had been moved. 'This lot is stacked differently,' Ann said.

Brionie needed only one glance at a sheaf of notes.

'We know all about that,' she said. 'It all had to be moved and re-stacked as part of a general search and after that we were told that a lady had wanted a good look at that settee at the bottom of the pile and Mr Waller had shifted everything for her but the upholstery was already too far gone.'

'The big fridge freezer seems to have been sold,' Tim said. 'There's a tatty old fridge in its place. A trade-in, I suppose. That swivel desk chair wasn't there before. I need a new desk chair. How do I make an offer?'

'You don't,' Ann said firmly. 'Leave it. I can fit you up better and cheaper from the stock in Dingle's furniture department and it won't have any woodworm in it.'

'Good God!' said Tim. 'I keep forgetting that you're now a woman of property. You never go there.'

'I don't have to go there often. I don't know anything about managing a multiple store and if I tried to do anything about it I'd surely make a mess of it. When I want something I just phone up and somebody brings it out to me, or I'm offered a choice of anything up to a dozen. The art of management is delegation,' Ann said pompously. 'I put Mr Hooper in as manager. He and Mum are back together. They're moving into Uncle Gus's flat. She can keep an eye on him for me. He was the only person I could think of with a family connection and knowledge of how shops work.'

'That sounds sensible. But we'd better audit him now and again. And again. He'll rip you off but he's not very subtle; we can make him cough up what he's taken.'

'I've already explained to him. He gets a salary and some commission but if he tries to help himself to anything extra he'll be subject to a deduction of twice as much. Mr Headstone was a great help. I think Mr Hooper got the message.'

They had moved on to where a pair of Welsh dressers supported an extraordinary variety of vases and other china. On the lowermost shelves were bowls, one of them by Wedgwood that Tim suspected of being valuable. These held all the ill-assorted trivia that had arrived as parts of larger lots. Among the lighters, cigarette cases and magnifying glasses were items such as dentures and spectacles that were so peculiar to the individual that Tim could not imagine them ever being sold, but Brionie said that she had asked the question and been told that such items were sometimes hired by the local repertory.

Brionie was looking over the same profusion of small artefacts. She was trying to compare the reality with the notes on many pages of lists in her hands and she was not finding the going easy. 'It says here that there were three cigarette lighters. I only see two.'

'Two is right,' said Ann.

'But against one of the three there's a note in a handwriting that only a genius could read. It seems to say "Cig B.", but it could be GG something.'

'For Cig B, try the cigarette box,' Tim suggested.

'Good thinking!'

The only cigarette box evident was a badly dented specimen. Brionie opened it with some difficulty and revealed what appeared to be a very small pistol. 'Ha!' she said. 'It looks like one of those lighters designed to look like a small pistol. It seems to have fooled my ignorant colleagues, but this one really is a pistol, presumably the one missing from the strong room in Mr Tirrell's flat. Don't touch it,' she added as Tim put out a hand. 'These things were difficult to unload and not much use when unloaded, so they often turn up loaded and primed.'

'Not this baby,' Tim said. 'Unlike the others this isn't flintlock, it's percussion and there isn't a cap on the nipple, so nothing short of a blowlamp's going to set it off – if, as you suggest, it's loaded. But I won't touch it. You'll want to check it for fingerprints, DNA and, in accordance with fiction, both fibres and pet hairs.'

'Somebody certainly will,' said Brionie.

'Well, the best of British luck to whoever it is. This may have been stolen from Ann's uncle but it's too small to have fired a heavy enough projectile to have knocked me out; and the flash and bang would have been noticed for half a mile round about.'

They prowled around for an hour without noticing anything more of significance.

FIFTEEN

Tim was due back at the hospital next morning for a follow-up appointment. He had been told not to drive until the doctors had pronounced him fully recovered, but nothing had been said against his being the qualified driver accompanying a learner. Ann had obtained a provisional licence and had jibbed at anyone but Tim being her instructor. They set off next morning, very slowly. It was her fourth lesson. They were a mile along the road before top gear was achieved. Umber, occupying her rug on the rear seat, was making sounds indicating impatience. She was expecting a walk and had been saving a full bladder in expectation but she had to wait until the hospital grounds were reached.

Dr Wainwright was her usual brisk self. With another doctor either assisting or supervising – nobody bothered to explain the relationship – she explored the recesses of Tim's brain and pronounced him at least as sound as the average man except for rare lapses in his ability to focus. The wound in his scalp had healed and there were already signs of some hair regrowth although he would have a small but permanent bald spot. The haematoma was shrinking. He was released with a warning to return if he experienced any of a dozen warning symptoms.

Ann was waiting on a hard stacking chair outside the consulting room. Her first concern was for the state of Tim's health and she made him repeat every word that the doctors had uttered before she was satisfied. She said that she could even learn to love his bald spot. She then told him that somebody else wanted a word with him and almost dragged him along the corridors to an office, near the chapel, where the supposedly but not always Reverend Mr Downing was waiting nervously. The pastor rose for a tentative handshake. When the two men sat, Ann did the same. Clearly she had no intention of being left out of whatever was to come.

The pastor had sought the meeting but now seemed lost for words. Tim felt obliged to speak up. The man was now, after all, a sort of connection – if not by marriage, by cohabitation. 'I feel that I owe you an apology for what I said the last time that we had a conversation. I should never have argued against your beliefs. And I never thanked you properly for marrying us.' Downing made a vague gesture, signifying that it was all part of a day's work. 'I hope,' Tim said, 'that the rubbish I talked is forgiven and, more particularly, forgotten.'

'Not forgotten, no. I've had time to think about what you said. I admit,' said Downing, 'that you did warn me. And I have had time to give thought to your words, and to consult my bishop. He suggested that, while I was not without sin, it was a sin that has dwindled in significance as society has changed and that my personal faith was a matter for my own inner conviction. He went over the known historical facts with me and agreed that there is much in what you said. Did you know that there are many other scriptures, giving a very different picture of Our Lord? I have always had to suppress an uncomfortable feeling that the ones included in the New Testament were chosen because they expressed the vision of Him that the Emperor Constantine's mother wished to be propagated.

'Anyway, I have to accept that there is no scientific proof of the existence or otherwise of a personal God. At bottom, therefore, it remains a matter of faith, which is where we started from. You had the grace to say that you preferred not to discuss religion for fear of damaging somebody's faith, so I felt that I owed it to you to say that my faith was shaken but is now recovering.'

Tim recognized the direction that Downing was taking and the gleam in the other's eye; and he knew for sure that the gentlemanly apology and assurance was merely leading up to a renewed attempt to imbue the pair of them with a matching belief in the improbable. To avoid the embarrassment of a sermon and the necessary evasion, he said, 'I had been waiting for an occasion to ask you a question. Almost as soon as Ann and I had met, it seems to have been generally known among her family that she might be conducting a relationship and also that she was likely to receive a substantial legacy. Please tell me how you received these two morsels of news.' The other's nerves had communicated themselves to him and his own words sounded pedantic in his ears.

Downing twined his fingers together in embarrassment. 'I don't know that I should . . .'

Tim let his expression show that his patience would not extend very far. 'None of you seemed to have any hesitation in giving the police a very inaccurate story about us. All I am asking is who told it to you. Was there a round table discussion? Or a series of phone calls? Or what? And do the police have the same information?'

'If they have it, they did not get it from me.' Downing's embarrassment increased although a mischievous smile made a brief appearance. 'I refused to speak up. In fact I may have allowed them to think that I was sheltering behind the seal of the confessional. I really couldn't believe that it was any business of theirs. But, on consideration, you have a right to know.'

He was answering Tim's question but he was speaking to Ann. 'It was the evening before the attack on Mr Russell, or so I understand. I officiate at two cottage hospitals as well as the infirmary so, as you know, I have a flat in the town. Mrs Hooper and I were still together although we were – ah – not broadcasting the fact of our association. Mr Hooper came to the door. They were good friends and your mother invited him in. She had known about Angus Tirrell's heart attack and death ever since it occurred and also the probability that you figured largely in his will. She had made genuine efforts to find you although there were limits to what she could do. She kept in touch with the police, of course, and watched the papers. Mostly, she was sure that you'd been raped and murdered and buried somewhere in the farmland.

'Mr Hooper was still quite friendly although his wife had moved in with me. I think that he found her absence a relief.' Mr Downing's face and voice revealed signs of exasperation. 'I am sorry to speak of your mother in this manner, my dear, but she has a great power to attract and ten thousand maddening habits that she cannot understand anyone ever objecting to. They were discussing where you could have got to and, even more importantly, what they could do to find you, when there was another arrival. This was that . . . that *person* Fogle.' Downing's face now expressed extreme distaste. He seemed unaware that he was also expressing uncharitable and indeed unchristian views about more than one of Ann's relatives. 'He is some sort of connection of your mother's, a second cousin I believe, and he stays in touch with her for the sake of occasional handouts. He lives only a few doors away from you, I think. He knew that she wanted to find you and he brought the news that you had moved in with this young man. To one of your mother's way of thinking, that could only mean the start of a serious – um – physical relationship and the handing over of control of any assets to the gentleman.

'I can tell you in all honesty that I was taking very little part in these discussions. I have no interest in worldly wealth. I was distressed to see the evidence of such greed among my close associates and remember saying so. Your mother expressed herself seriously offended at the implication that she was concerned with the money rather than with your well-being, but she spoiled her own argument by asking me, as a presumed expert on marriage, how one went about obtaining an annulment. She was also interested in knowing how long had to elapse before death could be presumed.'

Tim had been looking around the small office. From one or two high church items present it seemed that Downing shared the office with a Catholic priest and possibly others, but the austere nature of the room suggested that his claim to be uninterested in worldly goods was probably true. His grey suit was certainly off the peg and of no great quality. His shoes had taken the shape of his feet over many years of wear. 'This is all very interesting,' Tim said, 'but my wife's stepfather did arrive on my doorstep insisting that he had come to take her back into his protection. That's putting the most favourable interpretation onto what he was saying. What Ann's wishes might be didn't seem to interest him. There was a fracas in which he came out the loser, and shortly thereafter an attack was made on me which may well have been intended to be fatal. Did nobody drop a hint that life might be a little rosier if I were out of the way?'

'Heavens above, no!' The Reverend Downing seemed genuinely shocked. He spoiled the effect almost immediately. 'Not while I was in the room, anyway,' he said. 'I was tired. Mr Hooper – your stepfather, I suppose he is now again – did show an inclination to scowl when you were mentioned, but his attitude towards any other male person tends to be antagonistic. I could see nothing coming of their argy-bargy and I had no interest in the outcome. I excused myself and went to my bed. I could hear their voices for some time – until I fell asleep in fact.'

Tim was not wholly convinced of the pastor's veracity but it seemed unlikely that any of the others would have discussed murder or serious assault in the presence of a man of the cloth, however much lapsed might be his claim to virtue. 'One other person owed me a grudge,' he said, 'and that was Woodworm Waller. He might easily have been persuaded to have a go at me. His name wasn't mentioned?'

'Never in my hearing. And however much those people may have hoped that no marriage would take place, I prefer to consider their discussions as hypothetical. I really can't conceive of any of them creeping up behind you and hitting you over the head, which is how I understand that it happened.'

Ann had been listening in silence, her expression that of someone being told an unpalatable story from a doubtful source. Now she spoke up. 'But I'm sure you can conceive of one of them meeting up with someone else and letting slip how they wished that Tim wasn't around; and that person feeling obliged, by a past favour or a promise or a bribe, to . . . to take some action.' She groped for Tim's hand and reassured herself with a squeeze.

The pastor frowned towards the ceiling. 'Without knowing the persons involved,' he said, 'I can't give an opinion. I can only say that I couldn't rule it out. There are people within these parishes who might be so ruthless. I have been horrified by some of the evil deeds that have been committed and the thoughts that have been communicated to me . . .' His voice faded away.

'Thank you,' Tim said. 'I'm sure you've been admirably frank.' He wondered how to express a hope that the other's faith would soon be fully restored to him, but every form of words that he considered would have sounded terribly wrong. He shook hands again. Ann, who still nursed a grudge against her mother's lover, came away with only an unintelligible murmur of farewell.

As they walked to the car, Ann said, 'So anybody for miles around could have known that some members of my family might be grateful if you weren't around any more. Or even have thought, quite wrongly, that one of them would be grateful enough to pay a reward.'

Tim grunted in uncertain agreement, but once they had let Umber out of the car for another quick pee and had gone through all the complex manoeuvres that were required before Ann could actually set the car in motion he said, 'If that was the sort of reasoning behind the attack I think it's more likely that it was done with future blackmail in mind. But somehow none of it rings true. I'd be more convinced by a theory that whoever clobbered me did so because he owed me a grudge.'

'Mr Waller,' Ann said. She spoke absently. There was another car on the road, small in the distance.

'He owed me a grudge,' Tim admitted, 'and he was just the type to invent some sneaky way to clunk me secretly or from a distance. But then he was killed only a day or two later. I would love to think that I had an admirer so devoted that he or she struck him down in revenge –' from the corner of his eye Tim observed Ann, but no, it was unthinkable – 'but I'm not so vain as that.' For a self-indulgent moment he toyed with the thought of a devoted reader striking to preserve the life of his favourite author, but not even the egoism that drives the compulsive writer could lend the thought any credibility. He suppressed a small sigh for what might have been. 'I suppose it must be an outrageous coincidence. And yet my mind keeps turning back to Waller. There was something in his shop when we went back with Brionie.' Tim broke off. There was a bend in the road about a minute ahead. Once that was safely negotiated and the car had recovered Ann's modest cruising speed, he resumed. 'I was on the point of realizing what was odd or different but somebody said something that demanded my attention and when I came to think back I hadn't the faintest idea what it had been.'

As he spoke, an idea of what in Waller's shop had caught his attention paused on the threshold of his consciousness, but Ann, speaking slowly as befitted somebody driving a car for only the fourth time, said, 'And you're the man who always tells me to be sure that I say what I really mean. But you mean that you hadn't the faintest idea what it was in the shop that you noticed, not what somebody said that demanded your attention.'

Tim laughed but he was not going to allow her the last word. 'I'm also the man who tells you never to begin a sentence with "and" or "but". Even if I sometimes break that rule myself.' Ann took her hand off the wheel for just long enough to give him a playful slap on the thigh and the moment was gone.

'We're all being vague about Leo Fogle,' Tim said.

'Nobody has any real idea of his lifestyle, how he spends his time, where his finances come from and so on.'

Ann did not feel up to driving while trying to discuss so many topics at once. She pulled into a lay-by. 'Leo,' she said. 'He always seemed to be around but I never knew much about him. I think that the family tried to protect me from knowledge of such a disreputable character. He never tried to fit into society, make a contribution in exchange for his living. My father covered up his visits of supervision by saying that he just wanted to see that Leo was looking after himself. I knew, without really thinking about it, that Leo wasn't quite a proper person.' She laughed suddenly. 'After I took to the woods I used to see him sometimes, walking over the farmland, always smoking. In a way, his rural habits gave me a better opinion of him. I began to have a fellow feeling when I saw him, early one morning, slinking along with a dead mallard drake under his arm, which I supposed he'd snared on the pond beyond the farm buildings – the fellow feeling of one poacher for another.'

Ann was still speaking but she had lost the attention of her audience. Tim's mind had suddenly changed gear. Like a slow-motion computer it was following a chain of logic. There were hesitations in it, and even gaps where he knew that his input was guesswork rather than fact, but the overall picture was complete and satisfying. If one high probability was taken as factual, other pieces of conjecture suddenly became firm and credible.

'Drive on,' he said. 'I must phone Brionie straight away.'

SIXTEEN

Tim's problem with focus still made an occasional return and he was advised not to drive yet. Ann's driving lessons had been proceeding at as cautious a pace as did Tim's car when she was driving it, because he had been in the habit of fitting in a lesson only when he wished to be driven somewhere. On the day after his hospital visit, however, he had been unable to reach Brionie on the phone and, because he was becoming unsure of his reasoning, he decided to postpone speaking to her. His novel had reached a point at which a respite and a rethink before adding the final words would be beneficial, he had already made his routine visit to the gym and his garden was too tidy to require his services. When he asked Ann what she would enjoy, she surprised him. Instead of a tour of the shops and a meal out, or tea and sticky buns with one of her female relatives, she wanted a proper driving lesson. He made up his mind that she should have the lesson as well as the meal out. His presence at the tea with the female relative, if it ever happened, would be over his dead body. He was not inexperienced.

Ann's confidence was increasing. She no longer applied the brakes at the sight of a gentle bend or another vehicle. Tim was uncomfortably aware that the next stage would probably be a sudden rush of overconfidence but he persevered. They executed 'three-point' turns (in reality two- or four-point turns) in the open country and then turned back to look for a safe site to practise parallel parking. The first few such sites, where Tim would not have hesitated to park, were too tight for a beginner to attempt. The next was wider but would have entailed reversing around the rear corner of a gleaming Rolls occupied by a chauffeur who looked both able and willing to pick up any lesser vehicle that invaded his space and play it like a concertina.

Ahead and round a corner he spied an ideal space between the cones marking off a future excavation and a Lada so rusty that in the event of a collision the owner would probably have been grateful. They were, he noticed, almost outside the Waller shop. Under his careful direction Ann drove past the space. She was on the point of reversing, left hand down, when the rear door of Tim's car was suddenly jerked open and Brionie Phelps dropped onto the rear seat, pushing Umber aside and depositing what seemed to be a box between them. 'Drive on,' she said. 'Please, please, please,' she added.

Ann, already attuned to obeying instructions, drove on without quite touching the Lada. Brionie directed her into the car park of the only big supermarket and there she parked triumphantly. 'What the hell?' enquired Tim.

Brionie took a deep breath. 'I'm sorry to do that to you,' she said, 'but it's a very delicate matter and I need somebody local. I haven't been here long enough to know who's who. If I make the wrong move I could ruin my career and somebody else's. Do you see what I mean?'

She had gone on for long enough without saying anything. 'Either tell us what it's about or don't,' Tim said amiably, 'just as you like.'

Brionie gave an uncertain laugh. She was untidy and very dusty. 'Was I waffling? I'm sorry again. I'll spell it out for you. We've about finished at Waller's shop. Anything noticeably significant has been uplifted, samples have been taken and absolutely everything has been photographed. There are limits to the storage space available. So I was left here to go through the place for the last time, looking for anything significant that might have been missed. Woodworm Waller's next of kin – a cousin from Dundee – wants to sell off the remainder and dispose of the lease on the shop.

'I had done a thorough search, even moving some of

the furniture or crawling between to investigate the spaces down the backs of the cushions, and I'd upended the pots and vases. All that without finding a damn thing that had any relevance.

'I found myself looking at the big desk at the very back of the shop. It's all scratched and dented and infested with, at a rough count, three different varieties of wood-worm, so I'm in no doubt that it's been in the shop for some time and it's where Waller kept his records. In fact, we had found a lot of receipts and invoices and some barely literate correspondence in it. Anyway, I had seen desks like that before and they have all kinds of ingeni-ous hiding places. My colleagues had looked at it without finding more than one very obvious hidden drawer with some money in it. I wasn't convinced. I had seen a desk once that had a compartment with a false back and with another compartment behind the first one with another false back, and there were still drawers that slid out to the side from above and below it, so I was quite prepared for the tricks that the makers get up to. So I took a lot of measurements and located another space that didn't seem to be used for anything and I played with any move-able components until I found a way into that space.

'It was larger than you'd have believed from looking at the desk from outside and it contained some loose papers, all quite different in size, age and content. There were love letters and receipts and cheques and the draft of a political speech. Every one of them would have made somebody squirm if they had seen the light of day. Looking through them I could imagine only one thing in common between them, and that was that they could all be covered by the phrase "guilty secrets". I concluded that Mr Waller had studied every scrap of paper that turned up, down the back of a cushion or a drawer, in furniture that he'd come by in his business or as part of any haul of stolen goods that he'd bought; and I'd further concluded that he'd used anything compromising for a little blackmail.'

'Wow!' Ann said. 'Suddenly the question of motives for sticking a knife in him becomes wide open.'

'I haven't finished,' Brionie said. 'I then wondered if there wasn't another secret cupboard behind the first, and when I fumbled with it I found that what I had taken for the back of the space was actually this.' She lifted the box-like object onto her knee and lifted the lid. 'An expensive laptop computer. I was expecting a record of compromising accounts or correspondence. There was no attempt at secrecy, no password or anything like that, I just switched on and there it was, so I guessed that the owner of the computer had recorded some photographs for his or her own pleasure.'

'Porn?' Ann asked. She sounded more interested than Tim liked.

'Not Internet porn.' Brionie switched on the laptop and waited for it to boot up. 'But I'm not sure that either of you is old enough to view this material. Frankly, I don't think *I'm* old enough to look at it.' She keyed, glanced once at the emerging picture and turned delicately pink. Looking away, she said, 'There are several photos. Each shows a couple. The room is expensively furnished and the lady is wearing a great deal of jewellery that looks like the real thing – and far too much of it to be worn in public – and not much else. She is no chicken; I would guess a well-preserved and well-shaped forty. Her paramour is black. You'll see the position I'm in. There have been some serious leaks from the local police; some bobby has been selling tips to the media. If the woman is prominent or wealthy and I take these . . . do you mind?' She broke off. A woman with a curled mop of magenta hair was peering in through the car window with popping eyes. Brionie swivelled the computer away from the prying eyes. Ann, who had twisted round, managed to glimpse the picture and flushed scarlet.

'I don't think that old biddy could have made out enough to matter,' Brionie said shakily, closing the lid. 'She would have got around to looking at the faces last if at all. What I was saying is that if I bring these in and they escape into the media and the lady has clout, heads could roll, including mine.'

'What name is quoted as the licensee on the opening page?' Tim asked.

'Nothing very helpful.' The computer had shut down when she closed he lid. It took a few seconds to boot up again. Brionie read out a name and an initial. 'Does that ring any bells?'

'Common as muck, both of them,' Tim said. 'Of course, the surname on its own could be the name of our MSP but that isn't his initial.'

'Well, it wouldn't be,' said Ann. 'The lady would hardly be likely to use her husband's laptop to record a romantic adventure with the gardener or the milkman. She could well be the wife of the MSP or some other bigwig.'

'I think,' Tim said, 'that if you want our help you'll have to stop being so cagey. I have met the wife of our MSP. She came to open the new pavilion of the tennis club. She was about forty but still quite attractive and with a come-on smile. Let's see their faces. We won't tell tales.'

'I suppose that's reasonable.' Brionie looked around to be sure that there were no more prying eyes in wait before she brought up the pictures again and chose a shot in which both were facing the camera. She covered the lower part of the photograph with her incident book and turned the screen to where the two in the front seats could see it.

'Yes,' Tim said, 'proceed with caution. That is indeed the wife of our MSP. And the gentleman with her is an assistant librarian locally.'

'Thank you.' Brionie closed the lid of the laptop. 'That doesn't tell me what to do but it does tell me what not to do. I suppose I'd better seek an interview with some-body much further up the tree than my humble twig.'

'Yes, I think you had, and choosing with great care,' said Tim. 'And now, if that's all you want from us, we were going to practise a little parking and then give the dog a walk.'

'You'd better walk on eggshells,' Ann told Brionie. 'That one picture could furnish more than enough motive for both blackmail and murder. You may not have noticed quite how damaging those photographs could be. Was that what you'd call doggy position?'

'I suppose so,' Brionie said. Her voice sounded half strangled.

'Well you couldn't see either of her arms. I mean, she wasn't leaning on her elbows.' Ann was struggling but forged gamely on. 'Should we be discussing this with Brionie? She isn't married.'

'I am not a total innocent,' Brionie snapped. 'If you have something to say that is relevant, spit it out.'

'The lady's arms were behind her,' Ann said. She was looking up at the inside of the car's roof, refusing to meet the eye of either of her companions. 'She could have been reaching back to do something to the gentleman, but I think it looked more as though her hands were tied behind her. Not that she seemed to mind one little bit. I suppose . . .?' She turned her eyes and looked at Tim. It was his turn to redden. 'We can talk about it another time,' she said. 'Tell me, what is this thing men have about stockings and suspenders?'

'That's something else that we can talk about some other time,' Tim said. 'Preferably in bed.'

As Brionie opened the door to get out, her way was blocked by the return of the magenta-haired woman, who pushed her head and shoulders into the back of the car. She had a pointed nose, noticeably rouged cheeks and a fluffy artificial fur jacket. 'You should be ashamed of yourselves,' she said shrilly.

The intrusion was so abrupt and so obviously hostile that Umber, suddenly waking, made a sudden snap, inches from her face, and uttered a bark like the crack of doom. Tim grabbed her collar, settled her down and calmed her.

The woman jerked back, hitting her head with a crack

against the roof of the car. 'Set the dog on me, would you?' she exclaimed. Her voice had risen towards a screech. 'Gloating over pornography here, where bairns could have seed it. I've been waiting to get a good look at you and to take down the car's number before going to the police. There are laws about that sort of thing, you ken.'

Brionie kept her head. She could not leave the car because the woman's dumpy form was blocking the door opening as well as preventing her from closing the door. 'There are indeed laws,' she said with dignity, 'and I'll be bound that you don't know them. There is no law against looking at erotic material with friends in a closed and private car.'

'We'll see what the police say about that. I called them on my mobile and they'll be here in a minute. And I'm going to have that dog destroyed. Don't you touch that computer-thing. It's evidence,' she finished triumphantly.

There was more to come, but Ann was not waiting for it. She started the engine and drove forward, slowly at first and then more briskly. They heard a yell from the woman. Then the car's door slammed. There was a yelp from the tyres as Ann hauled the car round and they were bowling towards the exit. Ann wrenched the car to and fro, in and out of the thin traffic. Tim's fists clenched and he trod on imaginary brakes. The dreaded moment of overconfidence had arrived.

Ann's knowledge of the town's streets was better than that of either of the others. She swung off near Waller's shop into the empty car park behind a small former cinema, now a struggling bingo hall. There, behind a high wall still carrying the remains of a poster advertising a long forgotten film, they could not be seen from the street.

'Was that the wrong thing to do?' Ann asked in a shaking voice.

'No,' said Brionie.

Tim had had a moment to consider. 'You had to get out of there,' he said. 'If we'd waited for the uniformed officers, just what Brionie feared would have happened. Scandal. Publicity. Fury. Disgrace. Brionie can still save the situation.'

'Of course I can,' Brionie said doubtfully. 'How?'

'Keep a low profile,' Tim said. 'Use your mobile. Get hold of whichever of your bosses you can trust and beg for an immediate appointment. Go to meet him, alone, and tell him the story. Then it's his responsibility to decide whether to hush it up or open it wide.'

'And you?'

'We'll look after ourselves. Where's your car?'

'Getting its MOT,' Brionie said.

'Then we'll sit here. You use your mobile phone.'

'I don't think so,' said Brionie. 'And I can't use your house to hide in – they'll have your registration number. There's a café across the road with a quiet back room. I'll phone from there.'

'Good luck,' Tim said. 'We'll go home and face the music, if they follow us up. Don't forget us.'

'I won't. If you need a witness to say that she bit the dog first . . .' Brionie forced a smile, reached back for the computer and got out of the car. With a farewell gesture, she set off for the café.

'Now,' Tim said, 'I think we want Mr Headstone. 'You'd better speak to him. You're probably his richest client.' He dug in his pocket for his mobile phone.

When Tim's house had been broken into, it had taken the police several hours to answer his aggrieved phone call. He had not expected any more prompt attention on this occasion, but there was a blue-and-white car at his door within the hour. Either the lady with the magenta hair had some clout or the police were having an easier time of it. Fortunately, Mr Headstone was similarly free and had arrived with time for a brief conference.

The two uniformed officers were disconcerted to find a solicitor already present but Mr Headstone was quite equal to the occasion. 'Mrs Russell is the proprietor of

Dingle's,' he said blandly. 'I wish to discuss a few points regarding her inheritance so please do not take too much of her time.' When it comes to suppressing the truth or assisting an adversary to mislead himself, a lawyer is supreme.

The five – six with an accompanying dog – settled in the sitting room.

'May we know what this is about?' Mr Headstone enquired.

The lead constable coughed and said, 'We're enquiring into some allegations made by a lady. You are Mr and Mrs Russell?'

'Don't answer that,' said Mr Headstone. 'The officers are not being open about the object of their enquiries. We know nothing of the nature of these allegations, but they may be serious. They may concern others with similar names.'

'They are comparatively minor matters,' said the constable.

'Note my words and that answer, please,' Mr Headstone told the junior constable. He watched the younger man's pen.

The more senior of the two looked down unhappily at the dog on the hearthrug. He nodded towards Tim's computer on the table in the window. 'May we see what's on your computer?'

'Have you any objection?' Mr Headstone asked Tim.

'Not in the least,' Tim said. 'Apart from my writing it has nothing much in it except for our wedding photographs.'

'Ah!'

At the request of the more senior constable, Tim set the computer to boot up and then let them glimpse the contents under every reference in the menus of the main files and the memory stick. The only photographs, those of the wedding, had to be opened several times before the offices were satisfied that no erotic material was also included.

The radio attached to the collar of the more senior constable began to chatter. He went outside to reply. After listening for several minutes, he beckoned to his companion. The pair sat into the blue and white car. The car moved off.

Ann and Tim escorted Mr Headstone to his car. Mr Headstone's Dalmatian followed at heel and was settled on a rug on the back seat. Ann went upstairs to fetch Umber down from the bedroom.

There was a postscript to the story several months later. Tim had just got out of his car behind Dingle's, where he was to meet Ann, when the same woman reappeared in front of him. Her hair was now dark copper. Tim saw for the first time that she barely came up to his armpit. As an unmerited courtesy he leaned back against the wing of a Subaru and regarded her enquiringly.

'It's you,' she said. (Tim nobly refrained from making any of the obvious replies.) 'I dinna' ken how you managed to hoodwink the police but I'll tell you again to your face that you should be ashamed of yourself.'

'All right, you've told me to my face. Now tell me why.'

'You were gloating over disgusting photies.'

'Why were they disgusting?'

Tim's query was not intended to be provocative but stemmed from the genuine curiosity of the writer. He had been wondering for some time what criteria governed the average woman's susceptibility to disgust and how that might vary between places and ages. However, the woman appeared dumbfounded. 'They just were,' she said at last.

'Tell me this,' Tim said. He paused, wondering where to begin. 'I'm no artist, but suppose I did a pencil drawing or a painting of such a scene, for my own pleasure, not using real people and not showing it to anybody else, would that still be disgusting?'

She glared at him, suspecting a trap. 'Yes . . . No . . . You should be ashamed of yourself, bamboozling the police, and you with a young woman in the car.' She turned on her heel and retreated with short, quick steps. Tim noticed that her skirt was short and her tights or stockings were seamed up the back.

'That young woman was my wife,' he said after her and then wondered why he had considered that fact significant.

SEVENTEEN

On the following morning after being visited by the two uniformed constables, Tim felt on top of the world. Brionie's problems were not his problems; but the radio message and the sudden departure of the two constables suggested that somebody senior was calling off the dogs. The weakness following his injury and hospitalization was behind him at last. His legs were working freely and his sense of balance was quite restored. There was no pressure of work pending – he had emailed the finished version of his novel to his publisher the previous evening and was now at leisure until inspiration struck again. As they set off on Umber's morning walk through a cold, bright day, he found that the old pleasure of stretching his muscles and enjoying the sight of sunshine on landscape had returned. They walked further than usual, testing the bitch on some tricky retrieves of a canvas dummy.

As they neared home, their thoughts had turned towards coffee and a little relaxation in front of the fire; but from a distance they could see the shadow of a vehicle spilling from behind the house and as they got closer they found that Brionie Phelps had arrived again on their doorstep. Tim sighed – he had been looking forward to a period of recreation.

Brionie was looking distraught but determined. While trying to analyse her expression, Tim could only recall a lady speaker at a writers' conference that he had once attended. She had arrived at the rostrum wearing just such an expression. She had later confessed to Tim's mother that she had suddenly, and wrongly, become certain that the elastic had just reached the end of its reliable life.

Umber greeted her as an old friend. Ann left her in the

sitting room while she made her the cup of tea that Brionie evidently required. When she returned with it, the DSgt had tidied and more or less composed herself and was using the hall clothes brush to remove invisible dust from her uniform with jerky strokes.

Back in the sitting room, Tim joined them. 'How can we help you this time?' he asked. He tried hard not to allow any of the patient tone of a mother with a recalcitrant toddler to come through.

Brionie was staring vacantly into space but she pulled herself together. 'I don't think you can help this time,' she said. 'Not even God can help me now. I seem to be caught between a rock and a hard place. I mostly wanted somewhere to hide out while I try to think of something clever. I know that you can keep a confidence. I share my accommodation with a colleague who can't be trusted to keep her mouth shut – the original blabbermouth, she tells everybody everything – and I daren't go into the office at all. I'm just not ready to break this news yet.'

'You're welcome to hide here,' said Ann. The statement seemed rather bald so she added, 'Would you like to talk about it? We can hold our tongues.' Tim, who had been about to suggest that Brionie should try the public library, gritted his teeth.

'Yes, that might help,' Brionie said. 'I feel a bit overwhelmed. For the moment, I'm walking tall. My colleagues are already busy chasing up every potential blackmail victim, looking for Waller's murderer but otherwise trying to be as unthreatening and reassuring as possible. Of course, if anything criminal shows up we would usually have to act, although we're allowed a little discretion when it comes to persuading a victim to give evidence against a blackmailer. There's no prosecution in this case, but when it's mere indiscretion we can look the other way. Doing my homework, I discovered that the lady in the photographs, although she keeps as low a profile as she can, isn't just her husband's wife, she's a power in her own right. Independently wealthy, a contributor to good causes, a magistrate and a useful member of a dozen busy committees. Including the police committee.

'I managed to see the Assistant Chief Constable yesterday afternoon. He was appalled at the risk of offending the lady and he congratulated me on my common-sense handling of the problem, that's what hurts now that I've blown it. He quite agreed that it was too . . . too "juicy" was his expression, too juicy a story to let loose in the cop shop. It would be all over the place in no time flat, and the lady, who has held her tongue in the past over certain stories that the police were happy to hush up, would be disgraced and furious. He would put a confidential note on a very confidential file, he said, and make a favourable comment on my record, but it would be tactful if he remained out of sight and let her believe that the absolute minimum of officers had seen the evidence of her . . . "frailty", to use his word again. So I was to go and see the lady privately and obtain her solemn undertaking to give evidence, when his killer comes to trial, that Waller had been a blackmailer. Given that assurance we could let her take her computer back and expunge the evidence of her misbehaviour. She could then invent some much lesser sin to explain the black-mail.

'I drew his attention to the remote possibility that, if she was being blackmailed by Waller, she, or perhaps a family member or a hireling on her behalf, might have done the deed. I could swear that his hair actually stood on end. He said that that was beyond possibility, that she was above suspicion and that I could put it out of my mind.

'So I drove to the house occupied by the lady and her family, feeling very much lighter –' Tim suddenly sat up and leaned forward. Then he sat back, frowning – 'as if a heavy weight had been lifted off me. But,' said Brionie, 'my intention had been to see the lady, ask for a private discussion and imply a little blackmail of my own. I just wanted to be sure that her evidence would be available when wanted. So I walked up to her front door with her laptop under my arm, and rang the bell. A butler opened the door, looked at me as though he would have preferred to direct me to the tradesmen entrance but instead told me that the lady was out, attending a dinner.

'I went home and had what will probably turn out to be my last good night's sleep for years. Again I rang the bell. I was expecting a maid or the butler to come to the door after a suitable delay and lead me into a sitting room while he or she went to find the lady. Instead, it seemed that the whole family was already on the way out together. Within a fraction of a second she opened the door herself – and there was no mistaking the lady in the photographs – but she was accompanied, almost hemmed in, by one rather patrician husband, a large son in his early twenties and two younger daughters.'

Brionie took a long gulp of tea. It seemed to give her comfort but not very much. 'I had barely had time to identify them before her eye lit on the computer and recognized it by the distinctive colour. There was one of those fraught instants while everybody's mind zipped around in different directions. "Oh," she said, "you've recovered it. Well done! I'll call in and attend to the formalities later." She had lost all her colour when her eye lit on the laptop, but she must be a very quick thinker, much quicker than I am. Before she'd got more than the first few words out she'd grabbed it out from under my arm and turned back into the house – to lock it away, I suppose, with the intention of wiping it clean later.

'"She'll be glad to get that back," said her husband. "It cost an arm and a leg." He probably spoke truer than he knew,' Brionie said with a hint of a smile. 'Anyway, she was back within seconds, pulling the door to behind her. "Thank you," she said, smiling in a strained sort of way. "I'll see you later and thank you properly. We must rush now." Her eyes were begging me, woman to woman, to say nothing to give her away, but I was still too stunned to say anything at all. And I'd been told to behave with discretion and not to make any waves, so what could I do? They got into a dashed great Mercedes. The lady was the driver. When the others were in the car but she was still standing up and looking at me over the roof, she gave me a warning frown and put a finger to her lips. Then she sat down and the car oozed off down the drive. What should I have done? What would you have done?' she asked Tim.

'Probably just what you did.'

'But I didn't do anything.'

'Exactly.'

Tim could well visualize Brionie being rooted to the spot by the sudden divergence from her neat plan; he could picture the formidable lady wiping the evidence of her 'frailty' (to borrow the ACC's word) and blandly denying that any such evidence had ever existed or that she had ever even heard of Woodworm Waller ('where do these people get their extraordinary names?'); and he could recognize how disastrous Brionie's situation could become. The Assistant Chief Constable had thrown the book away but, to make use of the only apt expression to come to Tim's mind in that hectic instant, if the Flymo passed over the dog turd the ACC would be unlikely to admit to such a huge breach of proper procedures. He would deny everything. It was tragic. Tim managed to keep a straight face. If his planned morning had to be disrupted, at least the interruption was not without an element of humour.

'It's the end of my world,' Brionie whispered. 'I'm finished.'

'Let's not give up just yet,' said Tim. 'Could you delay making any mention of not having her support as a witness until after your Assistant Whatever-He-Is has put his notes on the files? He would have to stand by them then.'

'Nice thinking,' said Brionie. 'But the ACC was so concerned that he said he wanted my report within two days.'

'If by some chance,' Tim said slowly, 'you could bring

in Waller's killer, perhaps with proof of all the black-mail, would that get you off the hook?'

'I believe it might.'

'Has the shop been cleared yet?'

'That's where I was before I bolted here. I was giving it a last look over. Waller's sister-in-law has been told that she can bring in another dealer and clear what's left.'

'Then let's get down there damn quick,' Tim said. 'But first, ring Leo Fogle or knock on his door. Can you think of any way to persuade him to meet us at Waller's shop?'

'In fact,' said Brionie, 'I can. The radio was stolen out of his old banger. He wasn't going to complain about it, but a beat constable saw it happen from a distance though he wasn't near enough or quick enough to catch the thief. There are still two unidentified car radios in Waller's shop. Fogle may not give a damn about getting his radio back but I can insist that he comes and identifies it.'

'That'll do,' Tim said. 'Make sure he comes, whatever you have to tell him. We'll see you there.'

The shop's window was still obscured but the screen inside the door had been removed and two figures could be seen poking without much hope or interest through what remained of Waller's stock. There was no sign yet of Brionie Phelps or of Leo Fogle. They parked behind a battered looking van and waited.

At last Ann said, 'Can you really do anything to help?'

'Possibly. If the evidence is still there. It was Brionie's own words that gave me the clue. Do you remember how she expressed herself when she said how much better she was feeling as she drove to the MP's house?'

'Yes. She felt better, as if a weight had been lifted off her. That was a bit premature, wasn't it?'

'Indeed yes. But she didn't use quite those words. She – hang on. There's our delivery driver at the loading bay. I want a word with him.'

Tim left the car, found a gap in the traffic and crossed the road. He engaged the van driver in urgent discussion.

Brionie's neat little car nosed into the side street and parked in front of them. It was followed by Fogle's ancient but still quite usable Ford Pilot. Fogle parked further along the street and began to walk back. He was as unkempt as usual. Ann saw Tim and the delivery driver watching him. The delivery driver said a few words. Tim broke off and hurried back across the side street.

'Leave Umber in the car,' he said. Umber was visibly piqued at being left in confinement but she had learned to accept such treatment.

Fogle, as usual, was looking just as disgruntled. He threw away a cigarette and followed them into the shop. While Brionie sent the two strangers, dealers sent in by Waller's sister, out to their van, Fogle expressed his grudge against the world. 'What's this about? I never did give a damn about that car radio, I hate music while I'm driving and the tone wasn't good anyway.' He took a quick look at the two car radios on a shelf of the Welsh dresser. 'Neither of these was mine. You'd think the idiots would know that they're the wrong polarity for an old Ford. It's a poor lookout when a girl cop can burst in on you and practically drag you out to look at some rubbish—'

'Just as you were about to give yourself your medicine for the day,' Tim said.

'What?' Fogle seemed disoriented. His eyes were flicking to and fro.

'You've been here before, of course.'

'No, never. What are you getting at?'

'The van driver across the road loads here at least once a day. He recognized you. He says that he's often seen you here. You can smoke if you want to,' said Tim.

'But I don't—'

'I think you do.'

Brionie had joined them. She was looking puzzled but she was prepared to trust Tim, her only hope. 'So do I.'

Tim put a hand in his jacket pocket as though

feeling for a cigarette packet. 'Do you have a light?'

Fogle made the instinctive reciprocal gesture, putting his hand to his pocket, but then he withdrew it again quickly. 'Sorry, I don't.'

'I think you do. You're a compulsive smoker. You'd never leave the house without matches or a lighter.'

'You want a lighter?' Fogle stooped towards the bowl on the bottom shelf where the two lighters, one Dunhill and one Ronson, shone silver. Tim held him back with an arm across the chest. Fogle realized suddenly that his sins were finding him out. He attempted an impatient push and then a blow, but neither was effective. He found himself lowered to the floor, with Tim sitting on his chest and gripping his wrists.

'If you have gloves or an evidence bag,' Tim said, looking up at Brionie, 'I suggest that you feel in his right-hand jacket pocket. When you used the word "lighter" it came back to me. I had a good look through the place when we came to look for goods that Waller might have gypped Ann over. I didn't look particularly at the lighters – we were looking for larger stuff – but I was left with a mental picture and it wasn't of those two silver-coloured ones. At our wedding, when this person lit up, there was something familiar that didn't quite register at the time. It was of a lighter, not a very expensive one, which I had seen in here on my previous visit. It must have been losing its shiny finish and getting rusty, because somebody had given the rusty bits a rub with emery paper and then dressed them with copper sulphate. That, in case you didn't know, leaves a finish of copper on ferrous metals and I think he'd then given it a coat of lacquer.

'It has been said – and I associate the comment with the James Mason part in the film of *The Flying Dutchman* – that all great art contains an element of the accidental. True or not, the effect was very pleasing and could easily have been mistaken for a piece of deliberate artistry though I don't know how lasting the finish would be.

When I saw it again on our wedding day, well, there were other bells ringing and I saw it without realizing that I had seen it in Waller's shop.

'I suggest that Fogle here was having a confrontation with Waller. On the same occasion he found that his lighter had run out of gas, so he simply swapped it for one that had plenty of gas in it, from that bowl. You'll probably get his prints and DNA off it and off one of the two lighters in the bowl. You'll find plenty of his prints then on the goods in here, though you heard him deny that he'd ever been in here before. You see, he's your burglar. He killed Waller and he tried to kill me.'

Brionie stooped over the pair on the floor. 'How and why?'

Fogle struggled, throwing himself from side to side in an attempt to unseat his captor, but Tim remained firmly in charge. When Fogle's energy was spent, Tim could speak calmly again. 'Ann tells me that Fogle used to have a drug habit but that the family subscribed to put him through rehab. All very benevolent, but the success of rehab is a long way below a hundred per cent. It's only a guess, but . . .' Shifting his grip he slid Fogle's sleeve up. 'Look!' The needle marks were unmistakeable even in the dimness of the shop.

Tim had one of those moments of absolute certainty. Instead of a theory he now had absolute knowledge. 'Rather than go through the agony of rehab again, Fogle pretended to be cured. Addicts can be very clever at covering up their continued addiction. But he was not employable. He needed money to feed his habit. He took to burglary, selling the small and valuable goods through Waller but taking also money and cigarettes, and he eked out his income further with a little poaching.' Tim looked up at Ann. 'You had been browsing through my copy of *Hamlet*,' he said, 'and when you burnt your finger on the iron you quoted a few words. "The slings and arrows of outrageous fortune."

'"Slings"! That made me think. Poacher's weapon.

David and Goliath. In the pocket, no more than a piece
of leather and two cords, and then you've got just what
you need to propel a stone with great velocity. So that's
how.

'*Why* is less easy. But both as a burglar and as a poacher,
he'd be largely nocturnal. In fact, I think his habit on his
chosen nights was to go out at dusk, avoid the streets,
walk around the town in the farmland and return about
dawn. He would not want to walk the streets at night and
attract the attention of the police. But I'd told him that
it was my habit to walk the dog at dusk and dawn. That
would cramp his style. I suggest that he was leaving home
through the farm and saw me in my garden. He had the
sling, there were stones galore lying around and he gave
in to a sudden temptation to get me out of his way.'

Brionie bent down again and put a gloved hand into
each of Fogle's coat pockets in turn. She came up with
a lighter just as Tim had described it, a crumpled cigarette packet, a tangle of cord and a disc of leather pierced
with two holes. Feathers of various species fluttered to
the floor.

Outside the shop, Umber sensed that violence was
imminent. She began to claw at the car's windows, seeking
the weakest point. The car shook on its springs.

'Regarding the death of Waller,' Tim said, 'I can only
suggest that between a thief and his fence there must be
enough tension to start a war. It would only take the fence
to rip off the thief, which must always be a temptation,
and the thief would have little recourse except for
violence, which would be very likely to follow. It should
not be difficult to find the evidence.'

There was silence in the shop. Brionie was thinking it
over. Even Fogle seemed to be waiting. Then, 'Leo Fogle,'
Brionie said, 'I am taking you into custody on a charge of
attempted murder. Other charges will follow. You are not
obliged to say anything . . .'

EIGHTEEN

For years, Fogle must have been aware that some day he would slip up and then he would hear a variant of those words, yet the words seemed to spur him into fresh and frantic effort. He heaved himself up and tried to buck Tim's weight off, but Tim held grimly on. At last exhausted, Fogle went limp but his eyes glared into Tim's face, expressive of hate and fury. Mentally, Tim filed away a few words of description. There would come a day when one of his novels would call for eyes so filled with hostility. 'You moved your head just as I swung at you,' Fogle spat out. 'Otherwise I'd have hit you squarely. I'd have burst your brains. God, how I wish I'd killed you.'

'If it hadn't been me, somebody else would have fingered you,' Tim said.

Outside in the car, Umber was becoming desperate. Tim had left a rear window slightly open for her benefit and this seemed to offer the only hope of escape. She forced her jaws into the space and used them as a lever. It was agonizing but some little voice that sounded very like that of her master kept telling her that she must get out at all costs.

Handcuffs in hand, Brionie stooped over Fogle. 'You admit attempting to murder—?'

'I admit nothing. I deny everything.' Fogle's voice had become a scream. But he had had a few moments of rest. When he saw the handcuffs he was again spurred into a spurt of endeavour. At the same moment Tim moved and shifted his grip to allow for the placing on of the handcuffs. The result was that Tim's grip and his balance were both upset. The two men rolled. Fogle had body strength built up by years of exercise, shambling around the farmland and using his sling, whereas Tim was not as fully recovered from his period of idleness as he had thought. Fogle heaved himself to his feet. Tim was pulled up with him but was shaken off and went down on one knee.

Meanwhile, Umber had gained an inch and then another. Twice she tried to force her way through the gap but failed. She made a third great effort to force the window down just a little more. This time, inch by painful inch, she squeezed through and plunged down to the pavement.

Using his renewed strength and calling on fury and desperation, Fogle twisted aside and swept up a heavy earthenware pot embellished with figures and landscape in bold relief and dark glaze. He swung it above his head, intending to smash Tim into the ground. He was pouring out a torrent of abuse using words and phrases that Ann had never heard before.

Ann waited. When she had seen Tim embattled she had seen him victorious, so she was confident at first that he could vanquish any enemy. When she realized that Tim was in real danger she started forward, more than ready to put herself in the way of the blow. Brionie was frozen in horror and moved far too late. Tim had used up his strength and could only await with bowed head the blow that would surely shatter his skull, finishing the work that Fogle had begun.

Several passers-by had been drawn to the open door of the shop by the sound of conflict and raised voices. Umber brushed through them. Her instincts were of the finest though her brain had never been quick. She had been taught that people were sacrosanct, never to be bitten, but her senses seized on the hate and fear that were colouring the air. The only two people in the world of even the least importance were exuding fear and the other man emanated hate and fury. She hesitated, but only for a microsecond. The hair rose on her back and with a growl such as Tim had never heard from her before or since, she launched herself. She was a flying missile ready and eager to deal death. Fogle tried to turn aside from Tim and to brace himself for the impact, at the same time guarding his throat against the teeth that flashed in jaws already bloodied by their forcing of the window. His balance gone, his strength wasted, he brought the heavy pot down, not aimed at the man nor the beast but somewhere vaguely around or between them.

The pot missed both Ann and Tim, grazed Umber's head but took her in the hip, smashing her to the floor and shattering; but the moment was enough for Brionie and Ann to gather their wits. They threw themselves like furies at the now demoralized Fogle. In a demonstration of spontaneous, unrehearsed teamwork they slammed him against the wall, jerked his wrists together and applied the handcuffs. He was still swearing in a manner that would have shamed a porter in a fish market and Ann, as a relief to overstrained feelings, was repeating some of his more extreme phrases, apparently without conscious volition or any understanding. The detached portion of Tim's mind that always remained insulated from the action thought that the building might have to be exorcised.

Tim was down on the floor, nursing Umber's head, ignoring the pool of blood that was spreading under him but holding closed with his fingers the pulsing wound in her thigh made by a shard of pottery. The bitch was moaning in pain but drawing consolation from her master's touch.

The cluster of spectators in the doorway had grown, its members regaling each other with a dozen different versions of what had occurred.

The vet tidied up the broken hip but was unable to save Umber's leg. He suggested putting her to merciful sleep but Tim would have none of it. He knew about recovery. Umber was patiently nursed back to full health. She taught herself to walk again, to run and even to jump the lower fences. Before Leo Fogle even came to trial she had retrieved her first pheasant.

She is slowing up now. Her jowls are grey and she would as soon lie in the sun. When her time is up, Ann and Tim are agreed that her ashes will lie in her favourite place, almost exactly where Tim fell down, not far from the kitchen window.

In accordance with unvarying routine, Ann and Tim had spent many hours waiting between interviews during which they answered the same questions over and over again. Eventually they signed statements that include many of the answers given and also some material added by the various interviewers. It must all have made sense of a sort because, much later, Leo Fogle was convicted on all counts and sent to a prison which, by all accounts, he much preferred to the world outside.

When the taking of their statements was finished, the couple found themselves more or less at a loose end. Umber was able to walk with them, although so soon after her amputation her movements were clumsy, walking with the forelegs but hopping on the hind. She made very clear her refusal to be left behind so they all set off together in a longer but slower walk than usual, Umber carrying her favourite canvas dummy. Autumn was advancing and the first frosts had bronzed the trees.

They had gone past Ann's former bivouac when she suddenly broke a silence. 'I'm glad I'm not still living "beneath the greenwood tree".' She said. 'Enough was enough.'

'At the time, I thought you were going to refuse to come with me. Did you not trust me at first?'

'Because I let you walk on and then hurried to catch up? I trusted you. I didn't trust my knees. They went all wobbly at the sound of your voice.'

They turned to start back. Tim could not find a suitable comment on her revelation.

'What happens now?' Ann asked.

'The usual form would be a delay of months or years

while the lawyers prepare their arguments and the case comes to the front of the queue.'

'I meant about the book.' Evidently her husband's books were more important in Ann's eyes that the fate of her second cousin.

'Much the same except that the argument is over the title and details in the text.'

They stopped at the corner of the stubble field. Ann threw the dummy and then sent Umber to collect it. Umber lolloped out and brought the dummy back, her tail thrashing with joy at being back close to her real métier.

'When will you start another book?' Ann asked.

'When an idea hits me. Give me a start.'

'You give me a first sentence and I'll give you the next one.'

'All right.' Since hearing what Ann had been exclaiming during the fight with Leo Fogle, Tim was reasonably sure that she would not be easily shocked. 'Try this. "From the first, true to his name, Christopher Pyle was a pain in the bum."'

There was a long silence. They were nearing home before Ann declaimed, '"When he was put to his mother's breast he didn't suck, he blew."'

They staggered the last few yards, helpless with laughter. Umber wondered what on earth had got into them.